VEX HARLOW

Copyright © 2026 by Vex Harlow

All rights reserved.

No part of this book may be reproduced in any form or by any electronic or mechanical means, including information storage and retrieval systems, without written permission from the author, except for the use of brief quotations in a book review.

This is a work of fiction. Names, characters, and places are products of the author's imagination. Any references to historical events, real people, or real places are used fictitiously.

Designations used by companies to distinguish their products are often claimed as trademarks. All brand names and product names used in this book and on its cover are trade names, service marks, trademarks, and registered trademarks of their respective owners. The publishers and the book are not associated with any product or vendor mentioned in this book. None of the companies referenced within the book have endorsed the book.

NO AI TRAINING: Without in any way limiting the author's [and publisher's] exclusive rights under copyright, any use of this publication to "train" generative artificial intelligence (AI) technologies to generate text is expressly prohibited. The author reserves all rights to license uses of this work for generative AI training and development of machine learning language models.

Proofreading and Formatting by English Proper Editing Services

*For the girls who were forced to grow up too fast.
Who survived the fire,
grew teeth instead of wings,
and still found ways to love.*

The Playlist

A FOREST - THE CURE
GIRLS - THE KID LAROI
I DID SOMETHING BAD - TAYLOR SWIFT
DO I WANNA KNOW? - ARCTIC MONKEYS
HOUSE OF BALLOONS/GLASS TABLE GIRLS - THE WEEKND
JAWS - SLEEP TOKEN
SUPERMASSIVE BLACK HOLE - MUSE
I'M YOURS - ISABEL LAROSA
DE SELBY (PART 2) - HOZIER
VEGAS LIGHTS - PANIC! AT THE DISCO
HEADS WILL ROLL - YEAH YEAH YEAHS
BLOOD//WATER - GRANDSON
ROUTINES IN THE NIGHT - TWENTY ONE PILOTS
EXIT MUSIC (FOR A FILM) - RADIOHEAD

CONTENTS

Content/Trigger Warnings		1
1. Locke		3
2. Arden		5
3. Locke		15
4. Arden		18
5. Locke		24
6. Locke		28
7. Arden		32
8. Locke		36
9. Arden		40
10. Locke		43
11. Arden		46
12. Locke		50
13. Arden		53
14. Locke		59
15. Arden		63
16. Locke		66
17. Arden		70
18. Locke		76
19. Arden		82
20. Arden		89
21. Locke		94
22. Locke		98
23. Arden		106
24. Locke		111
25. Arden		117
26. Locke		123
27. Arden		128
28. Locke		136
29. Arden		140
30. Locke		144
31. Arden		147
32. Locke		151
33. Arden		154
34. Locke		163

35. Arden	167
36. Locke	172
37. Arden	177
38. Locke	180
39. Arden	183
40. Locke	187
Acknowledgments	191

CONTENT/TRIGGER WARNINGS

This is a dark romance. Not the "I warned you" kind, but the "I'm warning you anyway because I care" kind. Although it won't occupy the darkest corners of the genre, it does contain dark themes that may not be for everyone. Please review the content warnings below and prioritize your mental health. Books are meant to be enjoyed, not endured.

Mentions of parental neglect
Drug addiction
Death of a parent (on page)
Sexual assault
References to sexual assault of minors (non-graphic)
Sex trafficking themes
Threats and intimidation
Blackmail
Date rape drug use
Manipulation
Violence and physical danger
Murder and death

Criminal activity
Gambling
Frequent alcohol use
Power imbalances
Depictions of exploitation and toxicity in Hollywood
Detailed sex scenes, which include (but are not limited to): Dom/sub dynamics, anal play, praise kink, face-fucking, and edging.

Chapter 1
LOCKE

Another day, another meeting with an overpaid narcissist. This one's panicking over the possibility of his affair hitting the press.

"Tell me again why you haven't gotten a divorce?" I ask.

He just stares at me as if I should already know the answer. "I love her. She's the mother of my children. I just want a little excitement now and then. How realistic is monogamy anyway?"

I arch a brow, shaking my head slightly. "Whatever you say. Although I think she'd be happier with a divorce and half your money."

"Well, I'm not here for your opinion," he scoffs. "Can you help me or not?"

People call me a publicist. Press agent. A fixer. Whatever makes them feel better about hiring someone like me. I cover up the messes rich men make when they think they're untouchable.

I make sure their dirty laundry stays buried... sometimes literally. Some might say that I'm the best Hollywood agent around. Others might say I'm just too far gone. I'm more inclined to agree with the latter.

"Come on, man." He pleads as a bead of sweat traces a path down his brow. "I need these tabloid reporters off my back. I know you can take care of them."

"They're just doing their job," I reply, indifference clear in my tone. "I have ways of convincing them to keep quiet, but it'll cost you more."

He lets out a long sigh, like he's been holding his breath. Rubbing the back of his neck, he replies, "Whatever, I just need this done soon."

God forbid the world finds out he's not the flawless, doting husband he plays on red carpets and social media. *I can't believe I came all the way to Vegas for this.*

And while I would love to see this particular asshole's entire world burn, he's paying me far too much to let that happen.

I turn to gaze out the floor-to-ceiling windows. I couldn't care less that this man looks like he's on the verge of a total mental collapse. All I can think about is that I have more important things to do right now. A good cigar, for instance, is a much higher priority.

I used to care about this business, maybe a little too much. Used to work around the clock, worrying about my clients and the money. But I can't say that I've cared about much of anything in years.

At some point, all the things that used to be exciting or unique about my life just became background noise. When you have the world at your fingertips, everything eventually loses its sparkle.

The kind of boredom I feel now has settled into my bones after ten years of watching the same people ruin their lives in the same ways. A decade of covering up the same messes.

Tonight will be no different. My brothers are dragging me out to another club opening. As if it could be any better than all the others we've seen in this city. Nate promised me a cigar.

I turn around and he's staring at me with his head cocked to the side, like he's expecting me to say something.

"Hello, did you hear me? Can we get to work?"

"Yeah, yeah. I'll take it from here. If you're done with your little pity party, feel free to go. My colleague will send you the invoice."

Chapter 2
ARDEN

The lights of Fremont Street never get old, at least not for me. The mix of old Vegas nostalgia and new luxury ignites something in me that I can't quite explain. It's a unique kind of magic.

Maybe it's because I grew up a few blocks from here and spent years roaming these streets. When I walk downtown, it feels like I'm back in high school with my best friend, dipping in and out of casinos sixty years older than us, to see if anyone would serve us a drink at the bar. I huff a laugh, shaking my head at teenage me and her terrible fake ID. There were some bartenders who humored us, anyway.

Or the time Lexi and I rode a double-decker bus around town, all day, for no reason other than we *could*. We got off here, at this exact spot, and walked the rest of the way home.

This part of the city hums with a warmth that feels alive, electric, even in its brokenness. The neon lights flicker against the cracked pavement and illuminate graffiti-covered buildings. The streets reek of spilled beer and cheap liquor, crowded with the faces of wanderers and the forgotten who haunt Fremont Street night after night. They're hardly noticeable among the raging sea of drunk tourists, but I see them.

Every corner, every flashing sign, every inch of this place seeps into my blood. This isn't just where I live. It's who I am. *It's home.*

Maybe that's why I still come here so often.

Maybe that's why I chose this club tonight instead of one on the strip.

That, and it's inside the newest 21+ playground in Vegas. A mid-century-inspired facade paired with the finest modern luxuries, down to an awe-inspiring rooftop pool. This place is hot right now, making it the perfect spot to find single, good-looking, and most importantly, wealthy men.

As a 25-year-old single woman, what else would I be doing on a Friday night? Knitting? *I think not.* I wish Lexi were here right now; it's been far too long since our last girls' night. But childcare is hard to find, so I'm flying solo.

Inside the casino, the usual assault on my senses begins. The suffocating scent of cigarette smoke, the obnoxious chimes of slot machines, and slow-moving tourists who make me want to scream. I weave around them and manage to catch an elevator right as the doors close.

The club is sixty stories up. I smash the button and take a moment to steal one last glance at myself in the elevator's mirrored glass.

I quickly comb my fingers through my long, black waves, check that my winged liner hasn't dared to smudge, and swipe on a fresh coat of wine-red lipstick. Pausing, I examine the freckles scattered over my peachy-beige skin. They always seem to pop more when the weather gets warm. I smooth down my black satin minidress, counting the seconds until I have a drink in my hand.

The doors open and — *damn*. This isn't the kind of club I expected. It's a rooftop bar that takes decadence to a whole new level.

Gold accents catch the dim lighting, casting everything in a soft glow. The entire space is sleek and mid-century modern, with plush seating areas, a marble bar, and an open patio lined with fire pits. It's exclusive, dripping with class, and the gold of my heels mirrors the warm gleam of the bar's accents. At least I dressed for the occasion.

I'm only here because a friend from high school is a cocktail waitress and snagged a last-minute reservation for me, but the second I step inside, I decide I belong here.

As I make my way toward the bar, I scan the room. Every table is occupied. Couples cuddle together, sharing appetizers and slowly sipping their cocktails; groups of men and women in business suits talk quietly at their tables, and a large group of women gathers in a corner booth.

The woman in the middle of the group is wearing a white minidress with fringe lining the bottom, a sash reading "bride" draped over her shoulder. The rest are in varying shades of pink and red. In front of them, the table is littered with shot glasses all sitting around a large heart-shaped cake. I steal a glance as I pass by. Someone scrawled 'Same penis forever' on it in bright red frosting. I snort out a laugh as my eyes wander to the floor-to-ceiling windows revealing a view of the rooftop patio.

A cluster of men sits at the largest fire pit, right in the middle of the space. Three of them, all in dark, expertly tailored suits.

One has sun-kissed tan skin and messy blond curls; his arm drapes lazily around a girl who looks like she just stepped out of a Barbie box: long, sleek blonde hair, a pink, very short dress, and matching stilettos that have to be killing her feet. She looks like she could be my age. She also looks *drunk*. The man she's clinging to is wearing a smug smile that tells me exactly what his plans are for the evening. I roll my eyes and shift my gaze to the other two.

They both have the kind of build that makes it look like their suits are hanging on by a thread, muscles straining beneath the fabric. Almost-black hair, slicked back. Strong features. They look like they might be related, but one looks several years older, judging by the strands of grey scattered throughout his hair and beard.

They lean forward, elbows resting on their knees, tilting close to each other as they talk. From an outsider's perspective, it looks like they could be planning something or maybe talking business.

The bearded one is sipping an amber-colored cocktail, and I can't help but stare as he leans back to run his fingers through his salt-and-pepper hair. A lock comes loose, hanging in front of his brow. His posture relaxes against the stone bench flanking the fire pit as he takes another sip. Something about him tells me he's not a man who relaxes often.

Interesting.

I slide onto a barstool and order my usual. "Vodka martini, extra dirty." When my drink arrives, I steal another glance toward the fire pit. His sleeves are now rolled up to his elbows, revealing permanently inked ones underneath. His eyes scan the patio for a moment before locking on mine through the window.

This is my moment.

I let my gaze hold his for a second before I slip away from the bar and through the door, feeling his eyes on me the whole way.

The entire city stretches beneath me as I stand at the rooftop's glass-lined edge. The sun has just dipped behind the mountains, leaving streaks of pink and orange blazing across the sky. I watch as the city glows to life below, feeling his presence beside me before I even turn to look.

"Martini?" His voice is deep and smooth. "Bold choice."

I glance up. His eyes gaze into my own, the same warm brown hue as the whiskey he's sipping. I catch the scent of expensive cologne — something woodsy with a hint of spice — and cigar smoke. More tattoos peek out from beneath his collar, teasing just enough to make me wonder what else might be hidden beneath that suit.

"Extra dirty," I say, shooting him a sly grin.

His lips twitch as if he's amused. "Not many women order it that way."

I swirl my martini and pop an olive into my mouth, my eyes never leaving his. "What can I say? I like it filthy."

The smile that follows is almost predatory.

I take a slow sip, letting the tension linger. The way he holds himself and the calm in his posture are almost unsettling, yet I can't look away. I let my gaze drift down the length of his body. *Expensive cufflinks. Designer watch. Italian leather shoes.* Making mental notes.

He's the first to break the silence. "Are you waiting for someone?"

I hesitate, weighing my answer, but decide to keep it simple.

"No," I say, shrugging. "Just stopped by for a drink. You?"

He lets out a half-hearted laugh and shakes his head. There's a hint of something beneath it I can't quite put my finger on, but he just mutters a clipped, "No."

I nod, taking another sip as I study him over the rim of my glass. "Do you have a name?"

"Lochlan," he says as he offers his hand. "Most people call me Locke."

I take the offer. His grip is strong and controlled, and it sends a shock straight through me that I wasn't expecting.

"I'm Arden."

He doesn't let go right away. His thumb brushes once against the side of my hand before he releases me. That wasn't accidental. Not subtle either.

"So, Arden, who 'just stopped by for a drink'..." His mouth curves at one corner. "You usually pick rooftops for that?"

I mirror his smile, easy and unbothered. "I like the view."

"Right," he says, eyes dropping to my glass, "and very dirty martinis."

I shrug again. "Everyone has their vices."

He studies me for a moment, really looking at me. Like he's trying to figure me out.

Then he tilts his head toward the fire pit where his buddies are failing miserably at pretending not to watch. "Care to join us?"

The stone bench flanking the fire pit is surprisingly comfortable as I sink into the open space Locke directed me toward. The younger dark-haired man sits on the bench directly across the fire, arms folded, eyes fixed on me.

The blond one leans back, smile widening. "Well, well, who is this?"

I raise a brow, giving him a slow once-over that makes it clear I'm unimpressed. "Arden. You?"

His smile doesn't falter. "Sebastian."

"And *I'm* Ashley!" the Barbie slurs.

Yep, very drunk.

"I've gotta say, it's rare that my friend here invites a woman to join us... or anyone, really. He's not the social type," Sebastian says as he jerks his head toward Locke, who is now sitting beside me.

"And don't even get me started on *that* one." He gestures to the man on his other side dismissively.

"Don't even start," the mysterious man retorts.

"That's my brother Nate." Locke leans in close as he says it, his breath grazing my neck. "His bark is worse than his bite," he adds, leaning in closer so only I can hear it.

Nate gives me one stiff nod, eyes narrowed like he doesn't fully trust me, though I haven't given him a reason not to. I meet his stare, hold it for a moment, then give him a quick wink before moving on. His jaw tightens.

I let my eyes roam the group, noting the subtle differences in posture and attention. Sebastian leans forward slightly, still amused. Ashley giggles at nothing in particular, leaning against Seb as if he's the only thing holding her up. Locke inches closer to me, lighting a fresh cigar.

"Well," I say, leaning in. "What are we getting up to tonight, boys?"

Hours pass in a haze of warmth and rounds of cocktails. The firelight flickers, casting soft shadows on the sharp features of the group. We talk, but not about anything that matters. Sebastian spends most of the time detailing his latest trip to Mexico on his father's yacht. *Why am I not surprised?* He's the first to leave, with Ashley's arm draped over his shoulder. I have a feeling that's out of necessity more than flirtation.

Nate follows soon after, mumbling something about a phone call he needs to make. I catch him shooting me and Locke an uneasy glance before disappearing into the crowd. As if he were trying to telepathically urge his brother not to do anything stupid.

But then, it's just Locke and me.

He's kept his distance all night, which is *respectful*, or maybe he's uncomfortable? I'm not exactly used to either of those, so I decide to test the boundaries. I rest my hand near his on the bench as I turn my attention towards the glowing city skyline.

He doesn't hesitate.

His fingers close around mine, warm and firm, as he tugs me closer, and his arm settles around me.

"Seb was right," he murmurs, watching the fire. "I don't usually invite guests out with us. But he's always telling me to loosen up." His eyes fall back to mine; his gaze is steady, and his dark lashes cast shadows over his sharp cheekbones.

The way my pulse skitters actually catches me by surprise. "And how are you feeling right now, Lochlan?"

For a moment, time seems to stand still, then he closes the short distance between us with a kiss, letting that be his answer. I pull back, breath caught in my throat, and whisper against his lips, "Do you have a room here?"

Locke's fingers are firm against my wrist as he leads me through the halls of the hotel, moving with a kind of quiet confidence that makes my stomach tighten. The elevator dings open, and as soon as the doors close behind us, he turns, crowding me against the mirrored wall.

I press up onto my toes, brushing my lips against his, just enough to make him want to chase me. A flicker of something dark flashes in his eyes before he takes my jaw in his hand, tilting my chin up. Then he kisses me. Hard. Like he's been holding back all night.

I feel him everywhere. His grip on my waist, the heat of his body, the way his other hand slides into my hair, tangling at the nape of my neck as he deepens the kiss. His tongue sweeps against mine, slow and controlled, like he has all the time in the world. Like he *enjoys* making me wait.

The elevator dings open again, and he pulls away just long enough to murmur, "This way."

He walks with purpose, like a man used to being followed. And I do. The suite door unlocks with a wave of a keycard and a quick *beep*, and when he pushes it open, I barely have time to take in the space before my back hits the door.

But, *fuck*, it's gorgeous.

Dim golden light spills from a chandelier hanging in the center of the room and reflects off a sleek bar and a mini-fridge stocked with top-shelf liquor. An electric fireplace flickers, casting soft shadows over the plush mid-century modern seating area and polished tile floors. I can make out the distant strip glowing against the night sky through the floor-to-ceiling windows on the opposite wall.

Classic aesthetic, modern luxury. It suits him.

His mouth is on my neck before I can say a word, teeth grazing the sensitive spot below my jaw, and a soft sound escapes before I can stop it. His chuckle is dark, almost smug, when he says, "Don't hold back."

I drag my nails over his suit, feeling the tension in his shoulders, the crisp fabric stretching to the max now. He presses closer, and I can feel just how much he's enjoying this. "Maybe," I murmur, my breath hitching as his hands slide up my thighs, "you should earn more."

His lips part against my skin, exhaling as a wicked smile takes over his face. Then, he lifts me in one smooth motion. My hands grip his shoulders, fingers digging in as he carries me through the suite. Past the fireplace, the dining table I was already dreaming about bending over, and straight into the bedroom.

He lays me back on the mattress, lifting my dress and throwing it to the floor, but he doesn't climb over me right away. He stands there for a moment, watching, letting the anticipation build between us.

When he finally leans in, his mouth trails down my sternum. He moves slowly, savoring every inch, and I arch up into him before I can even think about it.

"Impatient," he whispers against me, his breath hot on my skin. "Relax. I don't disappoint."

His lips trail lower, and I can't stop the shiver that rolls through me. My hands clutch his shoulders, breath hitching, pulse racing.

His eyes come back to mine, dark and unyielding, and that look tells me he knows exactly what he's doing.

I let myself feel it all. The heat, the intensity of his gaze, the unmistakable pull.

But I haven't forgotten why I'm really here.

I wake up with something warm and heavy against my chest. I open my eyes to see his tattooed arm trapping me beneath it. His breathing is slow and steady next to me. Deep enough that he might not stir if I'm careful.

Shit, what time is it?

It's still dark, but dawn is creeping along the edges of the horizon outside the window. My pulse hammers in my ears as I test the weight on me, careful not to move too quickly. My leg feels like lead as I inch it over the side of the bed, toes finally brushing the cool tile.

I roll onto my side, sliding away just enough to get out from under him, muscles coiled with tension. Every breath, every tiny movement, risks waking him.

Sitting up, I let a soft exhale escape, staying as still as possible.

I let myself slip last night.

I glance down at Locke, still asleep. His arm is stretched lazily across the bed now. His breathing is deep and steady. The comforter drapes low around his hips, exposing more of his fully tattooed back than I need to see right now. Gorgeous and, thankfully, still oblivious.

It almost makes me feel bad for what I'm about to do. *Almost.*

I push that feeling aside and scan the room. Spotting yesterday's dress on the floor, I tug it on quickly. On the dresser, I notice a few of his things, as if he'd emptied his pockets there before he went to bed. A watch, a tarnished gold chain with a cross attached that looks ancient, and a small folding knife.

The watch catches my attention first. It has a red silicone band and a chaotic face displaying exposed gears, with ticking hands and numbers printed directly on the glass. It looks more like something you'd get in a Happy Meal than at a high-end jeweler. But the brand name makes my heart skip a beat. **Richard Mille.** A watch worth more than most cars. *Bingo.*

I slip it into my bra along with the chain since I'm still in last night's dress and, unfortunately, don't have pockets. I palm the knife, just in case. *Too easy. I didn't even need to check the safe.*

Shoes in hand, I exit the bedroom and move toward the suite's exit, my bare feet silent against the tile. As I reach for the door handle, something catches my eye, stopping me dead. The entrance to another bedroom.

My body refuses to move an inch as I stare. *Nate? Seb? Which one of them is in there?* A flush creeps up my neck at the thought of what they might have heard last night.

I shake it off and carefully twist the handle, willing the hinges to stay silent as I slowly open the door. The moment I'm in the hallway, hearing the click of the door as it closes behind me, I run.

My heart pounds, but not from fear. It's the rush. The thrill.

I slam the elevator button down, step inside, and press 1. The doors glide closed, sealing me off from the suite. From Locke. From last night.

I pause in front of the elevator mirror, smoothing my dress and attempting to finger-comb my hair into something more manageable. Then, I slip on my heels and straighten my posture as I prepare for my walk home.

My gaze travels downward, and I pull out the watch, just for a moment, to admire it. I can't help but let a small smile creep across my lips.

Because this is what I do.

Chapter 3
LOCKE

Fuck. What was I thinking?

Inviting a girl here. Letting my guard down. And... she's gone?

I reach for the other side of the bed, but all I feel are ice-cold sheets. Part of me expected her to still be asleep, wrapped up in the blankets. I even had my "I'm heading back to LA" excuse ready to go. Instead, all I'm left with is a faint trace of her perfume on the pillow.

A quiet laugh slips out of me.

She left first.

Bold. I'll give her that.

I rub my eyes and sit up, noticing the sun high in the sky through the window. I overslept. Too much whiskey and the events of last night hit me harder than I thought.

I need a shower.

I step in, twisting the handle just enough to shock myself awake. The water needles down my skin; it clears the fog the whiskey left behind, but not the memory of her. Her nails making trails down my back, her mouth against mine, her arching into me.

Most women linger. Hoping for a second round, a breakfast invitation, some excuse to stay in my orbit a little longer. To take advantage of my status... or my wallet. That's why I stopped trying. But her? She slipped out as if she had never even been here.

I turn off the water and step out, feeling marginally more awake. My ego should feel fine about this. Hell, I should be relieved. But something about it doesn't sit right. No one has ever walked away from me first.

I quickly run a towel through my hair before knotting it around my waist as I turn toward the dresser. Still trying to wrap my mind around the audacity of this woman. My hand reaches for the watch I remember leaving here last night but brushes against smooth wood instead.

I shake my head. I really overdid it last night. The watch must be somewhere else. My eyes scan the room, snagging on every surface. The nightstand is empty, and so is the desk. Surely, I would have remembered putting it in the safe.

I blink, then blink again. My heart is hammering in my chest now. I left my cross right next to my watch last night, and my new knife. These aren't things I would carelessly misplace. I know where I left them, and now they're gone.

And so is she.

The realization creeps in, curling tight around my ribs, making it hard to breathe. She knew exactly what she was doing.

A low, humorless chuckle slips past my lips before I can stop it. I'm not angry. Not really. I'm actually kind of impressed. The sheer nerve she must possess to do this to someone like me.

The watch and knife are replaceable. The chain... that's different. That's a line she shouldn't have crossed.

I should be pissed; any normal person probably would've called the cops by now. That thought doesn't even cross my mind.

I drag a hand through my damp hair, letting my thoughts settle. Then I move toward the floor-to-ceiling windows, admiring the city stretching out beneath me and the beginnings of traffic in the morning haze.

Where did she go? The question gnaws at me, sinking in deeper with every second of silence. How far could she be by now? My jaw aches as my teeth clench together, and I pace alongside the massive windows. She thinks she slipped away. But no one slips away from me. At least, not for long.

That truth steadies me. I will find her. Because I don't lose, I don't get played. The tightness in my chest eases.

This isn't over. Not even close.

And I *will* see her again.

Chapter 4
ARDEN

I never go home with stolen goods.

I've made it a rule: get rid of them as soon as possible. No holding, no second-guessing. Too much temptation, and I don't bring my messes home.

So, as I walk out of the casino like just another girl who made a drunken mistake last night, I make a quick call.

"Hey, Milo. I've got something for you. Can I stop by?"

I'm at the pawn shop ten minutes later. This isn't a pristine, well-lit, polished storefront. No, this is the kind of place you don't walk into unless you know someone inside or you're desperate. The kind that makes you wonder if you'll make it out in one piece.

I push through the door, and the shop is dim, lit by a single buzzing and flickering fluorescent light overhead that casts everything in a sickly yellow glow. Shelves sag under the weight of old dusty trinkets and pawned junk that looks like it's been sitting here since the '90s. The linoleum floor is scuffed, sticky in places, and it smells like no one has opened a window in years. There's a narrow hallway in the back, and I make my way through it, past more shelves full of crap no one's even thinking of buying, until I reach the unmarked office door. This is where Milo does his real business. I push it open and step inside.

He's at his desk, cigar in hand. A steaming mug of coffee sits next to a glass ashtray as he leans back in his chair with his feet on the desktop, like he owns the whole damn city. He's in his fifties, if not older. His thinning gray hair is slicked back, and the fluorescent light catches on bulky gold rings as he lights a fresh cigar. A real old-school Italian motherfucker. I don't ask questions, but if I had to guess, I'd say he definitely has mob ties. That's nothing new in this town. He has to offload the goods somehow.

I set the watch and chain neatly on his desk. I keep the knife. It never hurts to have protection. Milo doesn't react right away; he just leans forward, squinting at the watch like he wants to be sure it's real. Then he picks it up, rolling it between his fingers, casual on the surface, but there's a sharp glint in his eyes.

"Well, good morning to you, too." His mouth twitches: half a grin, half a grimace. "You don't usually drop this kind of shit in my lap."

I smirk. "Should net enough zeros to make your head spin. The question is, will you have a buyer?"

He flips the watch once in his palm, and his thumb lingers on the bezel. "I move watches. Rolex, Patek, even Cartier if it ain't too hot. But this?" He exhales a puff of cigar smoke through his nose. "This is oligarch shit. It's beautiful... and it could be trouble. I'm willing to bet somebody important's already looking for it." He raises an eyebrow, waiting for my response.

I shrug. "So what? Call your guy."

Milo's snort echoes through the room. I bite the inside of my cheek to keep from laughing. "My guy? He would shit himself seeing this on my desk. The kind of people who buy Richard *fucking* Mille don't do back-alley deals. They got brokers. Lawyers. Insurance policies that are bigger than my entire operation."

He exhales, tapping the ash from his cigar into the ashtray, his free fingers drumming against the desk as his eyes narrow. He's thinking. I just wait. I already know the greedy bastard isn't going to let me walk out of here with this.

Then finally, "I might know someone."

I arch a brow. "Might?"

He waves me off. "A middleman. He won't meet with you; he's selective, but if anyone can move this thing quietly, it's him."

"Great. Call him. Let's meet up today."

Milo chuckles, low and humorless, rubbing a hand down his face like he already regrets this. "It's not that easy. He's got rules. You don't just walk in with a stolen Richard Mille and walk out with cash."

I narrow my eyes at him. "Then how the hell is this going to work?"

He leans forward, his voice dropping slightly. "You let me hold on to it. I pass it up the chain. If he bites, you get paid. But it won't be today."

I hate this. Every instinct in my body tells me not to walk away empty-handed. I hold Milo's gaze, my fingers curling into fists. "You know I don't enjoy leaving with nothing."

He shrugs, completely unbothered, taking another drag of his cigar. "And yet, here we are. You want top dollar? You're gonna have to play it my way."

I weigh my options. I could leave, find another fence, but who else has access to this kind of market? And right now, I'm more concerned about getting rid of this hunk of metal without getting jail time. I release a sharp exhale. "Fine. But if I smell bullshit, I'll make sure you regret it."

Milo grins, flashing a smile that is unnaturally white for someone with his habits. "Sweetheart, trust me, I don't wanna fuck you over." He sips his coffee. "I just wanna stay under the radar."

I leave with no watch and no cash to show for it, unease trailing me out the door. Deals like this don't sit well with me, but I'll play it his way for now.

I can hear Lexi in the kitchen when I finally walk through the door of our condo. It's nothing much, just an industrial-style loft downtown, with exposed ductwork, polished concrete floors, and quartz countertops. The faux-unfinished look almost reminds me of my mom's apartment, except this is intentional. Nothing like the places Lexi and I grew up in.

When we first moved in, we spent weeks poking fun at the fact that anyone dared to market the spaces as 'luxury' condominiums. We quickly realized that our much wealthier neighbors get off on living a 'modest' lifestyle.

For us, it's the perfect blend of the comforts of home, if you can call them that, and small luxuries we can finally afford. And it's the only place where the noise and chaos of the outside world can't seem to touch us.

The smells of bacon and coffee hit me first. Then the sound of a small voice, high-pitched and bubbling with excitement, drifts through the open space between the kitchen and living room and down the small entry hallway I'm walking through.

"Tía Arden! You're home!" Zoe races toward me, her ashy blonde curls piled into two bouncy buns that spring with every step. Her fair skin catches the sunlight, and her wide, excited eyes stay locked on me as she launches herself into my arms.

"You'd think I haven't seen you in a year!" I laugh, squeezing her close. "I missed you, too."

Lexi hands me a mug of coffee, still steaming. Her bright orange hair is pulled into its usual messy bun on top of her head, and her amber-flecked green eyes are shining as her gaze drifts past me towards Zoe. "Hey, kiddo, movie time in your room. Adults need a minute," she says with a grin.

As soon as Zoe is out of sight, she leans in, practically bouncing on the balls of her feet. "Story time! What were you up to last night?" she says, wiggling her eyebrows up and down.

I sigh and turn to the living space, sinking onto the couch. "What do you think I was doing?"

Lexi narrows her eyes in my direction. "Obviously, I know *what* you were doing. The question is, with *who*?"

"No one noteworthy," I shrug, lifting the mug to my lips.

Lexi tilts her head, shooting me a look out of the corner of her eye. "Uh-huh..."

I exhale sharply, giving up any attempt at being nonchalant. "Fine. I met a guy."

I hesitate. Not because I don't want to talk about him, but because I kind of do.

"He's not like anyone else I've ever met at a bar. Not some desperate trust fund idiot looking to impress a girl with his daddy's money...although his friend certainly fits that bill... but he had a presence. Control. Like he was used to people waiting on his next move." I shake off that thought, avoiding trying to figure him out right now. "His watch alone could probably net me fifty grand."

Lexi nearly chokes. "FIFTY THOUSAND DOLLARS?" She looks like she just had an out-of-body experience. "From one watch?"

I smirk and give her a slow nod. "I'm telling you. He was next level... in every way possible." I give her a quick wink at that last part.

Now she's hooked. She pesters me until I spill all the details, down to what I took from him and how I got out of his hotel room without drawing attention. When I finally finish, she just stares.

Shock? Amusement? Disapproval? Even I can't tell sometimes. Then, "Well, what was his name?"

I shift in my seat and mutter, "Lochlan." Taking another slow sip of coffee, "Lochlan... something. He didn't tell me his last name, actually, but he told me to call him Locke."

Lexi instantly snatches her phone off the coffee table and taps the screen furiously.

I scoff, "You're Googling him? Seriously?"

She doesn't even look up. "Uh, yeah? You robbed a guy who had an amazing suite, a watch that could resell for fifty grand, a knife on his dresser... and who knows what else was hidden! That's not some random rich dude, Arden."

I roll my eyes, stretching against the cushions. Trying to give the illusion that he was nothing more than another target. Even if absolutely everything felt different. "Lex, I always do this. He was just another—"

Lexi's breath catches, and she whispers, "Holy shit."

My heart instantly drops into my stomach. "...What?"

She slowly turns the phone around, holding it out like it's the final piece of evidence in a murder trial. Her eyes are wide, and her mouth hangs open in disbelief.

The bold headline at the top of the page reads, "Crisis King: How Lochlan 'Locke' Bishop Buries Scandals Before They Break."

The article is paired with a photo that looks like the paparazzi took it. Him stepping out of a sleek black SUV, his face half-hidden by his hand as he walks away.

I blink a few times, then squint. "No fucking way."

"Oh, fucking way!" Lexi squeals, continuing to scroll. "Owner of Bishop Strategies, private PR. Crisis management firm for the ultra-wealthy. He's the guy who cleans up celebrity scandals before they have the chance to hit the press." Lexi keeps reading, but I lose track of what she's saying, and all her words blur together.

I've stolen from CEOs. Trust fund babies. Tech bros. Tons of men too rich to notice, or care, when their wallets or suitcases were lighter.

But this? Lexi's right, he's not just another rich asshole. His whole life is about Hollywood glamour and celebrities. He has connections. He might even be dangerous.

I exhale slowly, setting my mug on the coffee table. "Shit."

Chapter 5
LOCKE

I stand across from Nate, watching him rub his temples and glare at me like I've just told him I lost millions at the blackjack table. The obnoxiously large kitchen island is the only barrier between us. Which is probably a good thing since I can see how badly he wants to punch me right now.

I scan the room, waiting for him to say something. The suite is nice, sure. But at this point, I've stayed in too many of these places to care. They all blur together after a while. Perfect. Polished. A facade. The only thing remotely interesting about it is the little thief that was here last night.

I shove that thought down, trying to ignore the fact that my clothes still hold traces of her perfume. Bright citrus mixed with jasmine and a hint of vanilla. I shouldn't enjoy it, so why am I?

Nate exhales through his nose, jaw tight. "Let me get this straight, brother." That last word, dripping with annoyance. "You brought a random girl from the bar back here last night. What was her name? Aiden? —"

I exhale sharply. "Arden."

"Yeah, yeah." He says, waving a hand in my direction. "You brought her here, fucked her, and then, sometime before you woke up, she slipped out with your overpriced watch, our father's cross, and your knife?"

I shift my gaze to the floor, rubbing the back of my neck. It's a little more embarrassing when it's all laid out like that.

Nate leans forward, bracing his forearms on the counter. "You couldn't keep it in your pants? Couldn't wait until the next Hollywood event to pick someone a little more... I don't know, suitable? You had to go for some low-life girl in Vegas?"

His eyes narrow as he continues his lecture. "And now you think you're going to hunt her down? For what?"

I keep my expression neutral. Maintaining the controlled mask I've perfected over the years.

I could lie. Tell him I'm just after the cross. That it's sentimental. Maybe that's part of it... but the truth is, I'm curious. I want to know why she did it, if she does this often, if she even hesitated, and if she felt the same magnetic pull toward me that I did toward her. But, even more than that, I think she might actually be useful.

When I finally speak, I do my best to keep my mask in place. "She might be exactly what I need for the Jaxon Wilde situation."

Nate blinks. Then laughs, a single, humorless chuckle.

"You're kidding." He shakes his head. "You want to hire her?"

He stares at me for a moment, waiting for a response, but I just stare back.

"You actually might be insane, Locke. You've truly outdone yourself this time."

Right on cue, Sebastian strolls in, completely unaware of the hellfire he's just walked into. It only takes him one glance between us to realize.

"Are you guys fighting again?" He stretches, looking obnoxiously refreshed for someone who drank half the bar last night. "Come on, give it a rest, Nate. Locke finally got laid. You should be happy! Maybe he'll actually be in a good mood for once."

Nate levels a very flat stare at him. Then at me.

He exhales sharply, pushing back from the counter. "Fill your idiot friend in. Then, let me know how you plan on fixing this." He grabs his phone, muttering, "Unbelievable."

He turns back to me, unimpressed. "You owe me."

The door slams shut behind him. Sebastian raises a brow at me, waiting.

I grit my teeth into a forced, razor-sharp smile. "Well," I mutter, "that went well."

Sebastian isn't just some idiot I keep around for entertainment. We've known each other for almost our entire lives. Our fathers ran their slice of the Irish mob together. Now they share a prison cell, while we take advantage of the money and connections they left behind.

That's why I need him. I deal in power and influence. I run with the people who pull strings behind the scenes. Sebastian? He knows the streets. He's not afraid of the people who learned to navigate them out of necessity rather than convenience. Even though his upbringing was the furthest thing from rough, he's always had a way of gaining their trust. When we combine our skills, this entire city belongs to us.

The head of casino security looks like he already regrets letting us into the surveillance room. He keeps glancing at the closed door, like he's waiting for someone to walk in. Or praying for it.

"You said she took something?" the man asks, voice gruff.

"Yeah," I reply. "A watch worth more than your entire camera system."

His jaw tenses, but he clicks through the footage anyway. He keeps glancing at Seb, who isn't saying a word. Just watching, arms crossed, eyes scanning the monitors.

A few minutes in, I spot a blur of black satin in the sea of flashing lights. "Stop, that's her. Back it up three seconds."

He rewinds. There she is, weaving through the maze of slot machines, casual and calm as if it's just another day. The doors glow with the blue light of dawn as she slips outside.

Seb moves closer, squinting at the screen. "What street is that?"

"First," the security guard answers quickly. "Looks like she took a right. Probably headed down Fremont Street."

"Thanks," I say, pressing a folded $100 bill into his palm. "For your trouble."

The moment we step outside, Seb pulls out his phone. "Calling in that favor. I need as much camera footage going south on Fremont Street as you can get. Look for the girl in the photo I'm sending now." He hangs up and sends the message as we walk.

Moments later, image replies start coming in. Grainy shots from traffic cams, hotel exteriors, even a convenience store. In one clip, they circled her. Another highlights a neon sign she passed.

I pull out my phone, zooming in on the map to trace her path with my finger. "This is the store she passed. There are three pawnshops within a few blocks of it. She definitely hit one of them."

Seb nods, looking over my shoulder at the cluster of red dots. "Then let's start knocking on doors."

I nod in agreement as we head toward the closest shop.

Chapter 6
LOCKE

The air inside the Treasure Trove Pawn Shop is thick with stale cigar smoke. Sebastian slouches against a glass countertop, letting me take the lead while he idly scans a case of overpriced vintage cameras. He's just here for the show.

I brace my hands on the counter before me. "I'll make this easy for you…" I trail off, giving him an opportunity to introduce himself.

"Milo," he reluctantly mutters, lifting his chin and exhaling a puff of smoke into the air. "And what are you yappin' about?"

I pull out my phone and place it gently on the counter. When Milo glances down, it's me staring up at him, smiling and holding a glass of whiskey. I zoom in on my wrist, giving him a clear view of what I came here for.

"You've seen this watch today, correct?"

Milo's poker face is shit.

His eyes flicker, just for a second, but I see it.

"Can't say I have," he mutters, his eyes shifting as he takes another long drag of his cigar.

Sebastian lets out a quiet chuckle. "That's weird. Because every other shop we visited said you're the only guy in town with the balls to even look at something that pricey."

Milo shifts on his feet, setting his half-smoked cigar in a nearby ashtray.

"Look," he sighs, lacing his fingers together. "Let's say, hypothetically, someone did walk in here with a watch like that. That would be a very hot item. The kind of thing you don't just flip overnight."

"Exactly." I shoot back. "Which means you still have it."

He stiffens instantly. "I don't —"

I raise my hand, cutting him off. "Don't lie to me, Milo. It's insulting."

He stares at me for a moment, narrowing his eyes. I don't move. I don't blink.

Milo sighs, letting his shoulders sag. "Fine." He reaches into his coat and sets the watch carefully on the counter. "Here it is."

I pick up my watch, turning it over in my hand and holding it up to the light. Just how I remember it. "I'll give you twenty grand for it."

"That's it?" Milo bellows, throwing his hands up in disbelief. "That's not even enough to cover my cut!"

Sebastian raises his eyebrows and steps toward the counter. "It's cute that you thought you'd get one. Better luck next time."

Milo taps his fingers against the counter, his mouth pressed into a tight line. "Why even pay? Just take it."

I lean forward slightly, lowering my voice to a near whisper. "Because you're going to call her. Now. Unless you want her thinking you pocketed more than your share."

The color instantly drains from his face.

Sebastian lets out a quiet chuckle, shaking his head as he moves again, joining me at the counter's edge. "What's wrong? Suddenly have morals?"

Milo shifts again, like he's weighing his options. Protect the thief or risk facing whatever consequences we decide to hand out if he doesn't do what we say.

"Look," he sighs, rubbing a hand over his face. "She's gonna be pissed. If you bump it up to thirty grand, it might go over a little better."

Seb barks out a laugh. "She's lucky she's getting twenty. Have her here in the next fifteen minutes or it goes down to ten."

Milo exhales sharply. "Okay. I'll call her. Just don't turn this place into a crime scene."

He grabs the shop's phone and turns his back on us to dial.

I slip between two shelves stacked with dusty stereo equipment, keeping a clear line of sight to the front door. Sebastian drifts toward the other side of the store, plopping a ridiculous cowboy hat onto his head as he makes his way to a crate of old vinyl records.

The shop is silent, aside from the hum of the cheap fluorescent lights overhead and Milo's uneven breathing. He keeps glancing toward the back storage room like he's considering hiding in there until this is over.

Sebastian breaks the silence first. "Relax," he says coolly, still flipping through records. "We're not here for you."

"That's what worries me," Milo grumbles.

Time drags on. A minute. Three. Five. Ten.

When the bell over the door finally jingles, Milo startles, the ashtray rattling against the counter.

She bursts through the door like she owns the place. Confident, quick, absolutely no hesitation. Her pitch-black waves hang loose around her shoulders, with sunglasses pushed up on her head.

She glances around, her eyes snagging on Seb, who keeps his back to her. She doesn't seem to notice me behind the shelves.

When she spots Milo at the counter, her expression sharpens.

"There better be a great reason for you calling me back here so soon," she snaps.

Milo clears his throat, then mutters, "Watch sold." He hands over the envelope of cash I just gave him.

"I thought you said it would take a while," she says, suspicion creeping into her voice.

"Yeah, well... things changed." He nudges the envelope toward her like it's a bomb ready to explode.

She picks it up, flips it open with one hand, and counts. She's quick, efficient; I can tell this isn't her first rodeo.

"What the fuck is this?" She spits. "I know that watch sold for more than this. Don't fucking play me, *cabrón*."

Her eyes never leave him as she moves behind the counter, jabbing the envelope into his chest. "*¿Tú crees que soy estúpida?* You think I don't know what that thing is worth? I work too hard to get ripped off!"

Milo holds up his hands slowly, expression calm, voice steady. "Easy, sweetheart. Trust me, that's all I've got."

She snorts in disbelief, stepping closer. "Don't make me laugh." She turns away from him and mutters, "*Pinche pendejo!*" mostly to herself.

From behind the shelves, I can't help the grin tugging at my lips. *Oh, she's a firecracker.* She's hot when she's mad, too. Somehow, it's even hotter that she doesn't know I'm watching. My eyes linger, dragging up and down her body as she peppers Milo with more Spanish insults.

She walks back around the counter, heading toward the door as she shoves the envelope in the back pocket of her skin-tight jeans.

Milo doesn't make much of an attempt to defend himself. Maybe he's feeling guilty.

But just as she reaches the door, he calls out, "I swear I didn't take a cut. That's all I got for it." He waits for her to glance back at him, eyes narrowed, before adding, "Just take care of yourself."

Then, she walks out the door.

I send Seb a quick text before following behind her.

ME

> I'll take it from here. Grab a car and wait for my call.

SEB

Better watch your back. She's vicious.

Chapter 7
ARDEN
the next day

The walk home from the park is normal. Zoe skips ahead, her small hand in Lexi's, giggling about something I'm only half-listening to. Something about the swings, or the ducks. Something innocent.

I should be relaxed, but I'm not. Since yesterday, something has felt off.

I try to shake the feeling as we enter the building and take the stairs up to our floor. Lexi is still talking, shifting Zoe's backpack onto her shoulder as she digs around in her purse to fish out her keys.

That's when I see it. A hotel keycard neatly tucked against the doorframe. On our front door.

I stop dead. Of course, Lexi clocks my hesitation immediately.

"What?" she asks, frowning.

I don't answer. Instead, I snatch the card from the doorframe and shove my hand into the back pocket of my jeans.

Her eyes narrow at me. "What was that, Arden?"

My pulse pounds against my ribs as I take the card out and flip it between my index finger and thumb. White words stand out on the black plastic: 'The Founder's Suite.' His room. His bed. That night comes flooding back, and I feel like I might be sick.

Lexi's face shifts, confusion giving way to understanding.

Her voice is sharp, clipped. "That's *his*, isn't it?"

I swallow hard and nod.

She exhales through her nose, jaw tight, "Okay, not to state the obvious, but that means he knows where we live."

I give her a blank stare. "Thanks, I couldn't tell."

Lexi glances over her shoulder and around the hall. It suddenly feels very empty and a little too quiet. My hand tightens around the key. "Take Zoe inside."

Lexi hesitates for half a second, her fingers tightening on Zoe's hand, uncertainty written in her eyes. Without another word, she nudges Zoe through the door, following behind quickly to shut it.

I don't move. I just stand there, heart hammering in my chest, listening as the latch clicks. Then, I turn slowly, and my breath catches in my throat.

He's here.

Standing in the stairwell at the end of the hall. He's leaning against the wall, arms crossed, watching me with that unreadable expression of his. *Has he been there the whole time? Was he just waiting for me to notice?*

The air suddenly feels thicker. I lift my chin, fingers squeezing the key card so tightly it digs into my skin. "Stalking me now?" I call out to him.

Locke pushes off the wall, slowly creeping toward me. "Not stalking," he answers casually, "just waiting."

My stomach tightens.

He's getting too close now. Close enough that I can see how his gaze drags over me, slow and completely shameless.

"Breaking into my building?" I challenge.

"Who's breaking in?" He lifts his eyebrows slightly. "There's no crime in walking through an open door, is there?"

I exhale sharply, rolling my eyes at the audacity of this man.

Locke tilts his head, like he's still trying to figure me out. Then he smirks. "You're not running," he muses.

I refuse to let my expression shift. "Should I be?"

His smile widens as if he's enjoying this. I don't give him the satisfaction of looking away. But inside, my pulse is a fucking war drum.

He's here, in front of me, and my body remembers every second of our night together with brutal clarity.

Locke comes to a stop, inches from me. Then, before I can react, he yanks the key from my hand. The movement is jarring. His fingertips graze mine, and it's enough to make my skin burn where he touched it. He holds the key between his fingers, studying it for a moment. Then, slips it into his pocket with a soft chuckle.

"I had a lot of thoughts about what I might do when I confronted you." His voice is smooth, almost venomous. He tilts his head slightly. "Some of them weren't very polite." A grin tugs at the corner of my mouth. I can't help it. He wants control of this moment, but he's not the only one who knows how to play this game.

So I step closer, just enough to test the tension. To stretch it even tighter. To remind him he's not the only one who enjoys a thrill. "You?" The sarcasm in my voice shatters the thick silence. "Not polite?" I tilt my head up, giving him a broad smile. I hadn't quite noticed how much he towered over me until now. "Well, what made you change your mind?"

His gaze flicks lower, slower. I wonder if he remembers that night, like I do. Can he still feel my skin under his hands?

I don't move.

Neither does he.

For a moment, it feels like time folds in on itself. Like there's nothing but the air between us, thick and crackling with electricity. Seconds tick by. He doesn't look away. Doesn't fidget, doesn't soften.

Then he says, almost like it's a simple fact, "I think you might be useful."

I go completely still, my brow furrowing. "Useful?"

He doesn't rush to explain. He lets the word hang between us, watching me like he's waiting to see what I'll do with it.

"I'll explain," he says, tipping his head slightly, eyes catching the fluorescent hallway light. "Over dinner."

I let out a sharp laugh. Is he actually serious?

"Dinner?" I repeat. "With the man who literally stalked me to my home?"

His jaw tenses, and he lets out a short, humorless breath. "You keep saying that like you didn't rob me first."

My mouth snaps shut. *Okay, fair.*

He shrugs, his smile fading into something sharper. "But sure. If you want to call me a stalker, go ahead."

I narrow my eyes, tilting my head slightly. "How do I know you're not planning to kill me?"

His grin is smug and annoyingly confident. "You don't."

I shouldn't find that amusing. But somehow, I do.

I hesitate for a brief moment. Then, before I can overthink it, I whip the condo door open. "Don't wait up!" I call over my shoulder.

From inside, Lexi gasps. There's a beat of silence, then, "If you get kidnapped, I am not paying the ransom!" I close the door with a laugh.

Should I be laughing?

Locke watches the entire exchange with amusement glinting in his eyes. He steps aside, gesturing down the hall. "After you."

I roll my eyes, but step ahead of him. I don't know why.

I don't know what the hell I'm doing.

All I know is that I want to see what happens next.

Chapter 8

LOCKE

I have to admit, it was amusing seeing the shock wash over her face when she realized I was there. Waiting in the stairwell like some kind of psycho. *Am I some kind of psycho?*

That's something I've asked myself one too many times.

I push that thought aside as we approach the diner. Arden insisted we walk, not drive, as she led me to the nearest hole in the wall. I can't blame her for not wanting to get in a car with me after that stunt. I'm still following her as she walks through the grimy double doors and straight to a corner booth near the back of the restaurant. *Interesting, she wants us secluded.*

We take our seats on opposite sides of the booth; she claims the side facing the door. Her eyes scan the small restaurant, alert to every movement. She's on edge but calculated. She looks like a woman who knows what she's doing. I get a sense that she's noted where the exits are, and even with the diner's hum around us, she's ready to bolt if she needs to.

A server comes to the table with a coffeepot already in hand and the smell of stale cigarettes riding her clothes. She doesn't smile as she asks, "Coffee?" We both nod as she pours two cups, drops two laminated menus, and disappears back toward the kitchen.

Neither of us is eager to break the silence. So, I stay quiet, studying Arden's face.

She's radiant. A few freckles scatter over her warm, honey-toned nose and cheeks. Her black hair flows in effortless waves past her shoulders, occasionally falling into her eyes. A minor distraction she casually brushes aside. And those eyes, a piercing shade of blue, stand out above all her other features. Every detail, even that slightly crooked grin that lifts her soft, full lips, works. She's stunning, but not in a perfect, untouchable way. It's effortless. Real.

Her brow furrows. "Why are you looking at me like that?" I realize I must look crazy. Again. I snap out of it, shaking my head, and finally find my voice. "I brought you here so we could chat about a minor problem I'm having with a client."

"Oh?" She leans back in the booth, crossing her arms. "And which celebrity has fallen upon such misfortune that you need help from someone like me?"

That stops me mid-thought. "Wait, how do you know what I do for a living?"

"Let's just say I know how to spot an easy mark," she replies, examining her nails as if she's already bored.

Her eyes flick up, and I suddenly feel as if she's cataloging every detail about me. Of course she is. I bet she's been doing it since the moment we met.

I regain focus, continuing, "My client... a musician... he's been making headlines a lot lately. Mostly for the wrong reasons."

She leans forward, resting her elbows on the table. Her eyebrows rise as if she's suddenly more interested.

"He got into a fight at an awards show last week," I continue. "It's been on every gossip site for days. And he used to be best friends with this actor. I mean, they were inseparable."

Arden gives me a confused look. "And that's relevant how?"

"Well, they're not anymore. The actor claims he has video proof of something bad the rock star did. Something that'll go viral the second it hits the internet. He's trying to ruin my client's career."

Arden's eyes narrow thoughtfully.

"And if that video gets out," I add, "his entire team is screwed. Including me."

She sits for a moment, staring straight ahead, her gaze drifting past me to some unknown point in the distance. Then her eyes go wide.

"Wait." Her voice is barely above a whisper. "Please tell me you're *not* talking about Jaxon Wilde."

I blink at her. "Did you hear anything else I said?"

She ignores the question completely, leaning forward with both palms flat on the table. "Jaxon. Fucking. Wilde?"

I sigh, rubbing my temples. "Yes, congratulations. You cracked the case."

She leans back again, looking like she's just won the lottery. But then her eyes go dark. "Okay... but how am I supposed to help?"

"I just need access to the actor," I say. "We have a history. There's no way he's letting me anywhere near him. I need someone to get close to him, gain his trust, and get access to his devices so we can delete the video."

She nods once, then tilts her head. "I'm not sure I actually want to know, but what's in the video?"

"Jaxon isn't positive, but he thinks it's a video from a drunken night at a club a couple of years back," I start. "An underage girl got mixed up with them, which is not unusual for this actor. He finds them everywhere he goes and loves to take advantage of their star-struck nature."

I pause, watching her reaction turn from vague interest to fiery rage.

"So, I guess the actor got some footage of Jaxon with this girl that could paint him in a poor light. He didn't give me any details. I'm actually not sure if he remembers. He claims it's a setup."

She nods again, taking everything in.

"And what if he's lying?"

"That's beside the point. He's my client. He pays me to keep his reputation clean. It's not my job to figure out if he's being truthful."

Her brow furrows, and she stares down at the floor. I guess she didn't like that answer, but it's the truth.

When she finally looks back up at me, I still see a flicker of interest in her eyes. "How much?"

I laugh, a wicked smile creeping across my lips. "See, that's the thing. I already paid you." I reach into my jacket to pull out the watch she stole from me two days ago.

Her expression doesn't change, but I catch a subtle shift in her body language. She tries to hide a sharp inhale. Her grip tightens around her coffee mug. Her throat bobs once, hard.

Those blue eyes flick over the watch, then to my face, like she's running the math on every mistake she's ever made.

I continue, "Consider it settling the debt you created when you decided to take something personal along with this."

She looks down at the table again. Is that guilt darkening her features, or confusion? I let her sit like that for what seems like an eternity before I finally speak again.

If this doesn't convince her, I'm not sure what will. "Come on, you want more than this, don't you?"

She looks me dead in the eye, maybe for the first time. "What the hell is that supposed to mean?"

I exhale softly. I know she's going to deny it. "You could've picked a hundred different ways to make money, but you didn't. You slip into upscale clubs and look for the best targets. The ones who have influence or any semblance of power. You don't even steal cash; you look for things that hold some weight."

I let the silence linger for just a moment. Long enough for her to feel it. Letting the tension build. "You don't just want money; you want a way in. A different life. More luxury, more power, maybe just more comfort. This is your chance."

She scoffs, but I notice the way her throat bobs. The way she clenches her jaw. "That's ridiculous. Not everyone wants to be like you."

I lean back against the booth seat, folding my arms across my chest. "Is it? Sounds like you're trying to convince yourself, to me."

Then I say the only thing I think might stick: "Work with me and you won't have to slip in anymore. You'll be part of that world. The parties, the travel. Where Wilde goes, I go. And where I go…"

I let her finish that sentence for herself and watch as the realization washes over her. I know I'm right. It's written all over her face.

Chapter 9
ARDEN

As I sit across from him in the grubby diner booth, my thoughts are all over the place.

He's talking so much, and I almost can't believe what I'm hearing. How dare he make assumptions like he knows me. This life has never been about anything more than survival. Maybe with a little vengeance sprinkled in.

It's how I clawed my way out of the pit I grew up in, how I help Lexi give Zoe a better childhood than either of us ever had.

And coercing me into doing his dirty work? It's low, especially for someone who acts so high and mighty. He oozes arrogance; every inch of him is insufferable. He's a complete asshole.

But he's also right. I stole from him. And I can't help wondering what he meant when he said I took something personal too.

That watch wasn't an heirloom. The knife looked new. I should be focused on his extortion, but I'm stuck contemplating whether it's the knife or the cross.

I know I have to say something. Give him some sort of answer. Do I really have a choice? What will he do if I say no?

"Can't you just have a hacker break into his files or something? Why do you need me?"

His eyes meet mine again, and the way my heart flutters into my throat makes me want to scream. Why does he insist on eye contact?

"Well, no, actually. It's not like in the movies. I have a colleague who can make everything disappear, but he needs an access point. Something already on the network. The easiest way is for someone to be there in person... maybe grab his phone. We just need his cloud files."

I nod at him again. Filing the information away while my chest tightens.

"Just don't fuck him."

I bark out a laugh. "What? I don't just —"

"That was not a joke," he cuts in.

The annoyance in his voice grates on me, but my curiosity wins. "Well, since you're so worried about it, who's the guy?"

He leans in, letting the silence stretch, clearly enjoying my curiosity. This man loves suspense. Finally, he grits out, "Luke Holloway."

"Oh...." I reply. Trying to keep the heat rising up my neck at bay.

His jaw twitches. He has to know what that name does to people.

"So let me get this straight," I say. "First Jaxon Wilde, now Luke Holloway, and you're telling me I can't fuck either of them? Am I allowed to look, or is that off limits too?"

Locke seems to note my sarcasm but still gives me a flat glare. "Please be serious for once."

"Hey, I just want to know the rules." I say, lifting my hands in mock surrender.

His expression stays flat. "So, we'll leave tonight."

"Uh, hello? I still haven't agreed." I study him, noticing his expression change. His eyes look darker. His grin is sharper than it was a minute ago.

"Well, you could always go to jail. You'd look great in orange."

I freeze for a fraction of a second. Suddenly my pulse is hammering in my ears.

Zoe... Lexi... I can't leave them. Not like this. My hands press against the edge of the booth, gripping harder than I realize, trying to anchor myself.

His eyes don't waver, and it's infuriating. Every inch of him radiates the arrogance I hate and fear all at once. He'll see through me if I flinch. I can't let him win that easily.

I swallow hard. My voice comes out quieter than I'd like, steady but wary. "So that's it? If I don't go with you, you're calling the cops?"

He leans back, eyes glinting like he's already won a game I didn't know we were playing. "You committed a Category B felony. That'll get you somewhere between one and twenty years. Don't forget the $15,000 fine."

My stomach is twisting into knots. I don't have a choice. He's taking me, or I'm going to jail.

"How long will we be gone?" I ask. "Lexi will be working. She needs childcare."

"Lexi... the roommate? So, you're not the one with the kid? Huh. You give off that vibe." He cracks a smile that's just as infuriating as everything else about him.

I'm not in the mood to ask what the fuck that's supposed to mean, so I continue, "Absolutely not. I'm the cool aunt. But I'm also the babysitter. I *really* need to know how long we'll be gone."

He studies me, eyes lingering on mine. "A month? Two? It's hard to say with this type of job."

"Oh, perfect. I'll just tell my best friend to pencil me in for 'indefinite disappearance.' She'll love that."

"A couple of months or twenty years. Take your pick."

I scoff, sliding out of the booth. "You're unbelievable."

I don't wait for a response. I stand, toss a few crumpled bills on the table, and walk out into the warm evening air.

I don't look back. He may think he's won, but I'm not done playing.

Chapter 10

LOCKE

I'm on her heels in seconds. This girl thinks she can keep me guessing, but she couldn't be more predictable. I'm looking forward to fully unravelling her, piece by piece.

During our walk back to her condo, Arden sends a text to Lexi, letting her know everything's fine, then goes quiet. The silence between us is heavy. I notice the pause in her step, the subtle shift in her shoulders. She's holding something back; I can feel it. That gnawing sense of unease creeps into my chest and won't let go.

Next thing I know, she's ushering me through the door to her loft and gesturing toward the couch. The cushions sink under me, soft and overstuffed, smothered in mismatched blankets and pillows. It's not at all what I expected.

The condo itself is modest, with polished concrete floors and gleaming stone countertops that are functional without being too sterile. It's not cluttered, but it hums with life.

Houseplants spill green across ledges below large windows, and the walls are peppered with crayon drawings and finger-painted flowers hung with strips of clear tape. The industrial touch of exposed pipes and air ducts somehow makes it feel even cozier. Every corner of this home speaks of routine, comfort, and a family trying to carve out something brighter.

A reality show plays on the TV. Teen mothers sobbing into the camera while their boyfriends prove they're allergic to responsibility. It feels absurdly on-brand for this place. Arden and Lexi must eat it up.

Scanning the space, I realize Lexi is nowhere in sight. I figure she's keeping her daughter away from me, and I can't say I blame her. I wouldn't trust me either. At least one of them has some sense.

When she finally appears, she's glaring. Unnaturally bright orange hair that fades to blonde at the ends is wrapped in a large bun on her head.

"Locke." I offer her a hand as I rise from the couch and head in her direction. She doesn't take it.

"I know who you are. I'm sure you already know my name, too." It makes sense that she and Arden are best friends; they share the same fiery spirit.

She doesn't have time to get another word out before Arden stumbles back in with a duffel bag that looks like it might cause her to topple over at any moment.

Lexi shrieks, "Holy shit, how long will you be gone?!"

Arden forces a smile. "I don't know exactly, maybe a month or two? But you'll manage. You only work a couple of nights a week. You've got a backup for Zoe, right? That girl from the club?"

Lexi's eyes flash. She doesn't look happy. She looks terrified, actually, but she nods.

Arden leans in, wrapping her arms around Lexi in a tight hug. I catch her whisper, "I just need you to trust me on this one," before letting go.

"If anything happens to her..." Lexi's gaze slices to me, "I will cut your fucking balls off."

"Noted," I say smoothly, though I take a few steps back, anyway.

Seconds later, Arden is in Zoe's room whispering her goodbyes. When she rejoins me, her eyes are glistening and her lashes are clumped just enough to give her away. For the first time, I see something unguarded there. Not defiance or sarcasm. Genuine emotion.

She makes her way toward the door, her duffel bag bumping against her leg with every step. I reach for it without thinking. "I'll take that."

She shoots me a look and rolls her eyes, but in a few seconds she's shrugging the strap off and handing it over anyway.

The bag is heavier than it looks.

We're out the door moments later, the night air thick and quiet around us. By the time we merge onto the freeway heading south, she's gone silent, staring out the window like she's already bracing herself.

For the first time since this started, there's no one else between us.

No waitress. No roommate. No exits.

Just me, Arden, and the road stretching out ahead of us. Dark, empty, and impossible to turn back from.

Chapter 11
ARDEN

The drive to L.A. is one I've made many times. Nothing to see here. Just a seemingly endless expanse of desert on both sides of the car.

If he were considering killing me, this would be the perfect time to do it. Maybe that's why I'm not quite able to relax. I've been on edge since the moment I got into this car.

I've also been... curious. My imagination has already conjured up tons of different scenarios about the glamorous streets of Hollywood and the world I'm about to step into.

Red carpets, high-end shopping, and glitter trailing everywhere we walk. The type of glamour you only ever see in magazines or late-night reruns. In my mind, Hollywood is glossy and intoxicating. I don't know if reality can live up to the hype, but I'm finally about to find out.

As we drive and I stare out at the dark desert, my mind continues to wander. What is Locke's house like? Or maybe he lives in a hotel suite like the one he had here.

Either way, I'm picturing bare white walls, cold tile floors, and absolutely no warmth. That seems fitting.

That's when I realize he hasn't actually told me where we're going or where I'll be staying.

"Hey, where are we going exactly? And what are our living arrangements going to be while we're working together?" The question makes my stomach flip. Not because of the job, or the possible chaos waiting for us in L.A. but because I'll be trapped in the same space as him for weeks, maybe even months. I'm not convinced I can keep my hands to myself for that long.

"We might travel a bit, but for the week, you'll stay at my place." He notices my wary glance and grins. "What? Afraid to share a bed with me... again?"

He's right. God, he's right. I can't stand his arrogant, insufferable ass... but the memory of his body pressing me into the mattress, the tattoos inked across those thick muscles, the way his hand sealed around my throat, how easily he wrung pleasure out of me like it was nothing. I'd be lying if I said I didn't want more.

I realize I haven't answered when he adds, softer this time, "Don't worry. There's a guest bedroom and a private bathroom. I may be a lot of things, but a scumbag isn't one of them."

"Thank you" is all I can manage to say. Those memories are still swirling around in my head, leaving heat crawling up my neck. I need a distraction. Any distraction.

"So, tell me more about Jaxon Wilde," I say, trying to think of anything to get my mind off that night.

Apparently, that was not my smartest move. Locke looks like he'd rather run the car off the road than talk about his rock star client.

He begrudgingly states the obvious. "He's a 20-something train wreck that could probably use a shower and should definitely stop playing into the rock star stereotype. You know, all this throwing TVs out of hotel windows, smashing guitars, and getting so drunk he can barely remember the words to his own songs? It's not cute up close."

"But *he* is very cute."

Locke shakes his head, chuckling to himself. "Every girl your age seems to agree."

"Can you blame us?" I sigh, trying not to swoon at the thought. "All that angst and self-loathing? The accent? It works."

I pause for a moment, looking out at the vast expanse of desert illuminated only by the car's headlights.

"Not to mention his personality. His whole 'fans are family' thing.

Most celebrities are so fake, you know? But not him. Every time he speaks, you can just tell he's being genuine. And the lyrics? God, it's like he's bleeding on stage for everyone to see. Yet somehow it makes you feel better about your own mess. He's reckless, sure, but it's kind of... beautiful? Like he's not afraid to set himself on fire just so the rest of us don't feel so alone."

Locke scoffs softly, eyes narrowing at the stretch of road ahead. "Wow," he says. "Maybe *you* should be his publicist."

Then he goes quiet. The silence drags on for miles, and I start to wonder if I struck a nerve.

His jaw flexes right before he speaks up again. "He's not a hero, Arden. He's drowning. Drowning himself in all the temptations of celebrity. Women, booze, drugs, power. All of it will eat a person alive if they can't control themselves. The only reason he hasn't disappeared completely is that people like you keep believing in him."

I wasn't expecting that response. I blink a few times, staring at Locke as he drives. Yes, Jaxon sings about struggles, heartbreak, and anger, but he's smiling and laughing in every interview. Cracking jokes on social media. Nothing in how he presents himself would ever hint at that level of self-destruction.

"Anyway... tell me about *you*. About Lexi. How'd you two end up living together? What does she do for work?"

His questioning snaps me out of that train of thought. "Careful. If you ask too many questions, I might think you actually care." Locke tries to hide the way the corner of his lip turns up but fails miserably. "We're stuck in this car for a few hours. Might as well get to know each other."

I consider that statement for a moment, then shut it down. "Nope. I don't talk about my past. Especially not with you. As for Lexi, she works in HR. Or porn. Can't remember which." I give him a shrug, redirecting my stare out the passenger window.

A few seconds of silence pass. I sneak a glance at Locke, and his jaw looks tight. He doesn't look angry... maybe frustrated? Annoyed? Which only makes me wonder what he really expected from me in the first place.

"Cute." The word comes out dry. He's not impressed. Not fooled by me. His eyes stay on the road, but I'm scared to look at him too closely for fear that he'll see right through me if he glances over.

"Most people at least pretend they want to be understood," he finally says flatly. "I thought maybe your speech about Jaxon was the start of us being real with each other, but if you'd rather lie than trust me with something simple, that's your choice. Just don't be surprised when I stop asking altogether."

Chapter 12
LOCKE

Her perfume fills the car, clinging to the leather, and to me. The sweet scent is intoxicating, and I'm not sure how much longer I can keep pretending it doesn't affect me. *Good thing I'm sitting right now.*

We finally approach L.A. and are greeted by an onslaught of bumper-to-bumper traffic. A sea of brake lights flaring in endless red lines. "Home sweet home," I say dryly, as the car slows to a crawl amidst the chaos.

Arden's been quiet since our clash earlier, but there's a spark in her eye now, faint but unmistakable, even as we roll to a dead stop.

This part of the city isn't glamorous. Industrial blocks rise on either side of us, with tacky billboards scattered between them, and a thick layer of smog clouds the sky. It's pure Gatsby, the ash heap before the golden lights of Hollywood.

I watch Arden take it all in. "What do you think?" I ask, half-expecting another smart-ass remark instead of the truth.

"Nothing I haven't seen before," she says coolly. "Lexi and I drove out here once, after graduation. The first night we slept in her car, in a grocery store parking lot, until a cop kicked us out. Spent the rest of the night parked at the beach, waiting for sunrise. The next night we found a club, met some guys, and did what eighteen-year-olds with horrible judgment and nothing to lose do."

Her voice flattens. "That's how Zoe happened."

A faint smile tugs at her mouth again. "Guess this town really left its mark."

I blink, then nod once. "That's... a hell of a souvenir."

She lets out a soft laugh, almost a sigh. "We were idiots, but somehow it worked out okay."

The rest of the drive is quiet, but not uncomfortable, just the silence of two people too drained to fill it. Despite the silence, my mind won't stop circling her. The fragment of her past she just shared, the pieces of her present I've already observed, and that first night I saw her... it all blends together. I picture us in the same bed again, even knowing she's nowhere near ready for that. Not when there's nothing in it for her this time.

By the time we roll through the gate and up the long gravel drive, her eyelids are drooping as she fights to stay awake. She almost looks innocent like this, lashes low, head leaning against the window. If I didn't know better, I'd think she was.

I shift the weight of Arden's overstuffed duffel on my shoulder as I flip on the entry light, then lock the double doors behind us. Arden drifts down the wide hallway leading into the living area. Slowing down to study the abstract art lining the wall — thick, violent strokes of black across large white canvases. She lingers for a moment, considering them, before moving on.

She enters the living room with a muttered, "Nice museum you have here." Still enough energy to be a smart-ass, I see.

"Make yourself at home," I reply, sweeping a hand around the space. Then, all at once, it hits me. She's right.

Looking around at the vast expanse of white and gray marble, the slate walls, the black steel accents... it feels cold. Sterile, even. The only touch of warmth comes from the yellow glow of overhead lights and sunlight that streams in during the day. I had never noticed before. Or maybe I just didn't care.

"Come on. I'll take your things. Your room is this way." I jerk my head toward another hallway to our right.

Arden follows, but there's a hitch in her step, a hesitation she can't quite hide. As we move down the hall toward the guest suite, her gaze flicks from the art on the walls to the doorways we pass, cataloging details, locating exits. She's always alert. Braced for what might come next. I wonder what etched that instinct into her. Maybe it's just the reality that she's alone in a stranger's house, with a strange man she met twenty-four hours ago, who also tracked her to her own home. We didn't exactly start on the right foot. I can only hope that having a space of her own will convince her she can feel safe here.

At the end of the hall, I nod towards the door. Arden gently twists the handle and steps inside, her eyes widening as the room opens up around her.

A king bed enveloped in a white down duvet dominates the center. Across from it sits a sleek wooden dresser with a flat-screen perched on top. An arched entryway reveals a long marble countertop housing the sink and vanity, a large steam shower, and a separate soaking tub. It was all designed with ultimate luxury and comfort in mind.

She spins slowly, taking it in piece by piece, until her gaze snags on the real showstopper: floor-to-ceiling glass windows showcasing the backyard, the infinity pool stretching the length of the estate, and beyond that, the glittering sprawl of city lights below.

Arden doesn't speak. Just drifts closer to the glass, staring out at the view like it's pulling her in. Then her eyes snap back to mine, a brilliant spark cutting through the calm.

"Up for a night swim?"

Chapter 13
ARDEN

I don't know why I thought a midnight swim with a near-stranger was a good idea. But this house, this view, the room... it all feels so surreal, like I've stepped into a dream. Yet somehow, for the moment, this is my actual life.

In that moment, standing in the guest suite, surrounded by sleek lines and luxury at a level I've only ever seen on TV, I decided I'm going to let myself have this. The travel. The job. Him. Whatever *this* is. Because I know it won't last.

I guess that decision is how I ended up here, floating in Locke's massive infinity pool, suspended above all of Los Angeles. I glide toward the edge where the water appears to spill straight over the hillside; the lights stretching endlessly below, the ocean a black, unknowable line beyond them. The water feels warm against my skin despite the cool ocean breeze drifting around me.

For a moment, I close my eyes and pretend this is mine. All of it.

The view. The stillness. A life where I'm not always planning an exit.

Then Locke slips in. He doesn't speak, just drifts closer and closer until he's leaning against the edge, mirroring my stance. Just feet away. For a while we sit in silence, both of us staring into the night.

It's the kind of silence that feels charged. Heavy, like the entire world around us is holding its breath. This always seems to happen around him. The feeling of the air getting thicker. The way my body forgets how to do simple things, like breathe.

I don't look at him right away, but I don't have to.

His presence presses against my skin, calm on the surface but humming underneath. Dangerous in a quiet way. The kind of danger you don't see coming until it's already too late.

"Is this what you expected?" he asks eventually. His voice is casual. As if we're not half-naked in the dark. As if the memory of the night we shared isn't still hanging between us.

I take a second too long to answer, willing my body to remember why I'm here.

"The pool?" I reply.

"The house," he says. "Everything."

When I decide to brave a glance, water is sliding down the hard planes of his chest, the black lines of his tattoos look sharpened and vivid beneath the surface. Intricate Celtic designs woven together over the length of his arms and torso. They're precise and controlled, just like every other thing about him. My throat goes dry.

"I didn't know what to expect," I say, and it's the truth. "I didn't really expect to be here."

His gaze doesn't leave my face. Not to look at my body, or the view, or any of the countless distractions around us. Like he's consciously refusing to look anywhere else.

A corner of his mouth twitches. "And?"

"And it's..." I search for the right word and come up empty. Thoughts and memories collide at once. Cheap apartments with peeling paint, nights spent shivering under thin blankets, learning young that nothing was ever guaranteed. "Different," I finish.

Something flickers in his eyes, like he heard everything I didn't say.

"Different doesn't sound like a complaint."

"It's not." I look back out at the city, leaning forward on my elbows over the pool's infinity edge. "It all just feels a little too easy to get used to."

His expression hardens. "That's how it gets you."

The space between us feels smaller now. Or maybe I'm imagining it. Maybe it's just the way his attention presses in on me, like he's using it to avoid something else.

For a split second, I want to close the distance. To see if the pull I feel is real. To find out if he's as dangerous as he seems.

Then, his knee brushes mine beneath the water. It's brief, maybe accidental, but I swear I feel a spark. A jolt of electricity that bursts straight up my spine.

He stills immediately. Doesn't pull away. Doesn't move closer. Just waits.

My breath is caught in my throat. My pulse pounds in my ears.

I push gently away from the edge, widening the space between us again. Not much. Just enough to make the choice clear.

It was only one night.

He was just a mark.

We *can't* do this.

I'm here for a job.

Locke watches me the entire time. Something dark and wild passes through his expression. It's gone just as quickly as it came, sealed away behind that infuriating calm.

"Careful," he says quietly. "This place has a way of making people forget themselves."

I force a soft laugh. "Trust me. I'm very good at remembering who I am."

His gaze drops then, dragging over my lips, my throat, the bare skin above the waterline. It lasts less than a second. But it tells me everything.

"Good," he says, voice rougher now.

He pushes off the edge first, his jaw tightening as he does it. He's creating even more space between us. Still, his eyes linger on me. For a heartbeat I want to reach for him, but I don't. I can't.

Despite the tension coiling between us, for now, I'm just floating. Letting the water hold me, letting the lights of the city, and him, fade into the night.

The next morning, the smell of coffee pulls me out of sleep. As I roll over to check the time, sunlight flashes off the infinity pool beyond the glass door, bright enough to make me squint.

I'm still here.

I'd almost convinced myself that last night was just a dream. That I'd wake up in my own bed to the sound of Zoe getting ready for school while Lexi packs her lunch.

But no, I'm here. Which means *he* must be somewhere in this house, too.

I swing my legs out of bed, my bare feet landing on the cool floor, and only then do I remember I'm wearing nothing but a lacy black thong. For a second, I toy with the idea of walking around like this.

Maybe Locke isn't even home. Doesn't he have some high-profile PR crisis to manage? I dismiss the thought just as quickly as it came, reaching for the silky white robe draped over a hook near the tub. I slip it on, wrapping the belt tight around my waist.

As I move down the hall, most of the doors are closed. Though one is cracked just enough for a sliver of warm light to spill across the cold gray tile.

I know I shouldn't snoop around other people's houses, but my curiosity gets the best of me, and I nudge it open just enough to peek inside. For a second, I'm caught completely off guard. I don't know what I expected, but it wasn't this. It's an office; it must be *Locke's* office, but it looks like it belongs in an entirely different house.

A massive wooden desk sits at the far end of the room. An open laptop is perched beside a small lamp that drenches the space in warm, golden light. A thick-cut crystal ashtray rests near the corner, with a small wooden box sitting next to it. Through the glass window on the lid, I can make out the shape of cigars stacked neatly inside.

Dark wooden shelves climb the walls, each one flooded with books. Most of them look old and worn, like they've seen centuries.

Next to the door, a stretch of exposed brick catches my eye. I reach out, half expecting it to be fake, but it's real, all right. Impressive... and surprising.

My attention drops to a sleek mid-century console sitting against the same wall. A turntable and two massive speakers sit on top, polished and waiting for someone to use them. Below, a sizable vinyl collection fills the shelves. I step closer and kneel, fingertips trailing along the spines. Johnny Cash, Tom Waits, Miles Davis.

He might just have a soul after all.

There's a sleek leather couch on the other wall with a small coffee table in front of it on which another cigar box rests. I'm noticing a pattern here.

I suppose it could all be for show, another prop in this carefully curated museum of a house. Still, I linger a moment longer before slipping back into the hallway, letting my fingers brush the edge of the turntable one last time.

When I reach the open kitchen and living space, I realize the morning light has changed everything. The sun streaming in through the massive windows gives everything a golden hue. The edges are softer, less sterile.

A small French press sits on the counter, a sleek glass mug beside it, the rich scent of coffee filling the air. Next to the coffee is an espresso machine with a sticky note attached: *I didn't know what you'd prefer, so I made coffee and prepped the espresso. Have whatever you like.*

I shake my head, smiling despite myself. A thoughtful gesture? This man keeps blindsiding me this morning. I pour myself a cup of coffee, swirling in some cream, and take a sip as I resume my hunt for the elusive, broody, but surprisingly, thoughtful asshole.

I spot him outside through the wall of glass leading to the backyard. He's wearing an immaculate black button-down shirt, tattoos barely visible beneath the collar, gray slacks, and another gleaming watch. He looks good. A little too good. *Remember why you're here, Arden.*

He's pacing the length of the pool, phone pressed against his ear, cigar in hand — seriously, at this hour? — and stress written all over his face.

He presses his fingers to the bridge of his nose, then drags them across his brow. His shoulders look tight. Whatever he's dealing with, it can't be pleasant.

The urge to watch him longer claws at me, but I force myself to turn away. The coffee warms my hands as I slip back toward the bedroom. Whatever today holds, I need to be ready for it.

Chapter 14
LOCKE

There's no sign of Arden except the missing coffee. Good. It buys me a few more minutes to ground myself.

My phone buzzes in my pocket, and I let out a sigh when I pull it out and realize it's Nate again.

NATE
Any updates?
Timeline's shrinking faster than projected.

ME
Working on it.

NATE
We don't have the luxury of delays.

ME
I said I've got it, little bro.

NATE
...Right. Yeah. Just keep me posted.

The pressure's mounting faster than I'd like; we have to move quickly to catch Luke before he does something stupid. Caution isn't a luxury we have anymore.

I know it's her when I hear footsteps coming down the hallway. She's light on her feet, but I can feel her getting closer like static in the air, crawling under my skin where I swore I'd never let another person again.

I turn just as she appears at the threshold to the kitchen, and for a moment, everything else falls away.

She's dressed to kill.

A black fitted dress hugs her like it was sewn onto her body, stopping mid-thigh. Her legs look longer than they are, toned and bare, carried on black leather boots with a chunky heel that thuds softly against the tile and adds a couple of inches to her height. Still, I'm at least six inches taller. Her makeup is sharp. Black liner cut into perfect wings, smoky eye shadow deepening the corners of her eyes, and her lips are painted a burgundy shade that looks almost the color of blood.

I drag my gaze up, past the hourglass curve of her waist, past the bare skin of her collarbone, until I meet those ocean blue eyes. She's smiling. Barely. Like she knows exactly what kind of wreckage she's leaving in her wake, and she's enjoying it.

"Coffee okay?" My voice comes out rougher than I intended.

She nods, offering a small smile before drifting closer. "Coffee was great. So was the music."

There's a glint in her eyes that's sharp, like she's discovered a secret. My gut tightens, but before I can unpack it, the buzzer at the front gate cuts through the room. Nate.

I curse under my breath. "We have company."

Her brow arches. "Fun."

I almost smile at her sarcasm, but there's no time. I hit the intercom and buzz him in. Minutes later, Nate strides through the door like he owns the place. Black jeans, a fitted leather jacket, mirrored sunglasses, and his motorcycle helmet tucked under one arm.

My wild younger brother: brilliant and reckless, and the reason this business still exists. Nate doesn't just work with me; he keeps the machine running. Cleans up messes. Handles things I can't, or won't, put my name on. Which means he's the one who takes the most heat when something goes wrong.

His gaze snaps to Arden instantly. Assessing and suspicious.

"Hello again," Nate says, his tone a little too friendly.

"Charmed, I'm sure," she shoots back.

Nate's eyes flick to the coffee in her hand. "You settle in fast."

Arden's smile doesn't waver. "Only when I'm invited."

He grunts, "We'll see how long that lasts."

I shoot him a look that tells him to stand down, then jerk my head toward the back patio. "Outside."

Arden lingers, leaning against the kitchen counter, swirling her coffee like she has all the time in the world. Casual. Unbothered. But when Nate and I step out, I catch her reflection in the glass. The tilt of her head, the subtle inching toward the door. She's listening.

I expected as much.

"We're moving forward," Nate says, lowering his voice. "Holloway will be at the gala next Friday. Not Wilde, though; he's on tour."

"Excellent," I reply. "Arden's coming with me."

Nate's jaw tightens. "I wouldn't be so quick to decide. Once you bring her out in public..." he exhales sharply. "You don't get to control how people spin it."

I give him my best reassuring smile, placing a hand on his shoulder. "Then let it spin. I'm not worried."

His jaw flexes again, but he lets it go. I can see he's not convinced, but there's no point in arguing.

"Fine." He hesitates. "And you're sure about her?"

"She's more capable than you think," I reply, sharper than I mean to. Nate seems to have forgotten that I've seen her in action.

She played me like it was nothing, slipped right past every defense I thought I had. If she can do that, she can handle this. Still, this isn't a club or casino floor. It's Hollywood. And it's an entirely different world.

I abandon that thought as we move on to logistics: venue, surveillance, and proximity. Behind the glass, I catch Arden's shadow shift, just barely. She's still there. I'd bet good money she's caught every word.

"I'll handle the details and prepare her for the onslaught of cameras and carefully practiced smiles," I mutter to my brother.

He doesn't want her near me or anyone else in this city. Certainly not in Hollywood. I can see the concern written all over his face.

Nate drags a hand through his hair. "Once you bring her into this world, you think she's just going to walk away like nothing ever happened?"

"She's not staying." I assure my younger brother. "Once this is done, she'll go back to Vegas."

It's a promise I don't entirely believe, but it's enough to keep him from pestering me further.

Nate studies me for a second longer. Then he exhales again. "She's here to help us with a problem; she'd better not become one."

I nod, because that's what he needs to see.

Through the glass, I watch as Arden sets her coffee on the counter and turns toward her room.

I don't know how much she heard.

Whatever it was, it must have been enough.

Chapter 15

ARDEN

I didn't hear the entire conversation, just fragments. Names. Places. I gathered enough information to let me know this event matters, but not nearly enough to tell me why.

Most of it blurred together the second it left their mouths. There was just one thing that stood out.

Arden's coming with me.

He spoke the words with an ease that told me the decision had been made long before he bothered to say it out loud. Locke stated it like a fact. Nate responded with concern for his brother's reputation, disguised as strategy. I wasn't a person in that conversation; I was a pawn.

And Nate's face? Tight-jawed and overly cautious, his gaze constantly assessing. It's clear that he sees me as just another liability.

Fair enough. I know I'm not here because anyone *trusts* me. I'm here because I'm "useful," as Locke put it.

Honestly, his suspicion tells me more than his approval ever could. Men like him don't waste that kind of scrutiny on people who don't matter. Whatever his reason, I don't have time to dissect it now.

And whatever this week holds, I have a feeling I won't have a say in any of it.

Two days later, I'm sitting at Locke's kitchen counter while he makes espresso like it's the most natural thing in the world.

The week hasn't been difficult, but it hasn't been comfortable, either. There's a constant awareness between us, like the air is humming with electricity. Every time we end up in the same room, it feels intentional, even when it's not.

Apart from that, it's almost like a vacation. Luxury estate, top-tier amenities, and apparently a personal barista.

"You've seriously never had espresso?" He's staring at me like I have two heads or something. "You've never had a latte? Cappuccino?"

I shake my head. "I never knew what to order, so I just stuck with regular coffee. If it ain't broke, don't fix it, right?"

"No," Locke huffs. "That's unacceptable."

I arch a brow. "*Unacceptable?*"

"We're fixing it. Right now."

He pours milk into a silver pitcher and places it under the steam wand. His movements are practiced and precise. I watch as he tilts the pitcher just enough for airy foam to form on the surface.

When he hands me the steaming mug, our fingers brush. It's nothing, barely a second, but my chest tightens anyway.

He doesn't pull his hand away immediately, doesn't look away either. His attention fixes on me with an intensity that makes the steam curling from the mug feel hotter.

"You're going to let it cool down if you keep staring at it," he says.

"You're the one staring," I retort.

"I just want to know if you like it," he urges, motioning for me to hurry.

As I lift the mug to my lips, his eyes stay locked on mine.

I watched him make the damn thing. There's nothing in the cup but espresso and milk, but the way he's watching makes my nerves hum. I consider asking why this matters to him. I decide against it.

"Well, you're right. That is delicious," I say, wiping a thin line of foam from my lips and setting the mug on the counter. "Next time, less milk."

He smiles a real, genuine smile. "Noted. I'm glad you liked it."

I give him a sly smile. "Thanks for a great first time."

A chuckle slips through his lips. "Keep saying things like that, and I might think you actually like me."

I shift my eyes away from his, looking down at the granite countertop. Damn it, I need to keep my 12-year-old sense of humor in check. I have no business flirting with him. This is a job. I'm an employee.

The smile fades from his face, and my thoughts are interrupted by his voice, low and serious once again. "You should get ready. We're going shopping."

"Shopping?" I repeat.

"Yeah. This gala isn't exactly a jeans and t-shirt event."

"Okay, then," I mutter as I stand to head back to my room. "Thanks again for the coffee."

He stays silent, giving me a half-smile as I head down the hall.

Chapter 16

LOCKE

Every afternoon this week has ended the same way.

Me and Arden in my office. Her on the couch with a book in her hands that I'm not sure she's actually reading. Me at the desk, tablet in hand, skimming headlines and drafting press releases while a record spins low in the background.

I suppose it should feel routine by now, but it doesn't.

I've learned her tells. The way she pretends not to listen. The way her attention hones when something matters. The fact that she never asks questions she hasn't already thought through.

The record spins out, the crackle fading into silence.

I try not to look at her. If I do, I'll read too much into how comfortable she seems. The way she settles in like this is a choice, even though I didn't give her one.

"So," she says, sitting up to face me. "What's this gala all about?"

There it is.

I keep my eyes on the tablet, unsure how much truth I want to give her right now. She doesn't need to know *everything*, just enough to do the job.

"It's a fundraiser."

"For what, exactly?"

I exhale through my nose. Of course she won't let that be enough.

"Mental health and addiction recovery. The industry's favorite virtue signal."

She snorts in response.

I turn the screen I'm holding toward her. There's an image of a man standing on a red carpet, smiling into the camera. His sleek blonde hair is perfectly styled. Baby blue eyes stare back at us, and his arm drapes around a tall brunette.

The headline above his image reads: *Luke Holloway's Charm is Winning Over Hollywood.*

Her reaction is instant. "Luke Holloway. Ever the pretty boy."

"Publicly," I say. "Privately? Not so much."

I feel the shift in her attention the second the words leave my mouth. The way her posture straightens and her eyes narrow.

"What do you know that you're not telling me?"

I open the wooden box on my desk, reaching for a cigar. More for the breathing space than the smoke. I clip the end before lighting it and taking a long drag, looking past Arden as I respond.

"Luke," I finally reply, exhaling a thin stream of smoke. "He takes what he wants. He has no regard for who it might belong to, or what that means for anyone else."

"That sounds personal," she says carefully, like she's weighing her words.

I glance at her then. She's studying me like there's a right answer and she's determined to find it.

"Men like him don't respect boundaries. They see them as challenges," I continue, ignoring the comment. "And trust me when I say he takes on any challenge that comes his way." I tap ash into the tray harder than necessary. "He's charming, though. People see only what he wants them to. He's very good at making his messes look like someone else's fault."

"So why doesn't anyone call him out?" she asks.

"Some have tried," I say. "They're the ones who tend to... disappear from the narrative."

Her eyes widen, but her silence tells me she understands exactly what I mean.

I change the image on the screen before she can ask another question.

This time we're looking at a very different image. Not a pristine red-carpet photo, but a gritty one of a man under blinding stage lights.

He's thin but muscular, wearing tight leather pants and no shirt. Sweat drips down his tattooed chest as he screams into a microphone.

His headline stands in stark contrast to Holloway's: *Jaxon Wilde's Partying Sparks Concern Among Fans.*

She scoffs as soon as she reads it. "That's bullshit."

I look at her again. This time I don't hide the interest.

She talks about his charity work, his fans, the way the press could've highlighted anything else about him, and I listen. Really listen.

I track every shift in her tone, the way frustration flashes across her face as she rants. I note what she emphasizes and what she dismisses. She speaks like someone who's been paying attention long before this job came into the picture.

"So, you see what's happening," I state plainly.

She gives me a silent nod. "One of them is *actually* dangerous, and the other just looks like it... and the media has both of them wrong."

I draw on the cigar, smoke curling between us. "Most people just believe what they're shown." I hold her gaze. "Not you, though."

She exhales, shaking her head slightly. I can see it on her face. The discomfort, the realization that this is only the surface. She looks like she's already tired, though we haven't even started yet.

"If Luke's as bad as you make him sound," she mutters, "I can't wait to ruin his career."

I glance at her then. Long enough to know she isn't speaking lightly; she means it. Even if she doesn't yet understand what that would actually cost.

"Trust me, Arden," I say evenly. "You don't want to see how deep the corruption goes. I wouldn't want you to, either."

She watches me for a moment before smirking. "Keep making comments like that, and I might think you actually like me."

I don't respond.

I just study her. The confidence, the grit, the way she keeps pushing even when she shouldn't. I hold her gaze a moment longer than I should.

Then I turn back to my work.

Chapter 17
ARDEN

"You clean up nicely... for a thief," Locke's voice drifts in from the bathroom doorway, smooth and dangerous and threaded with amusement.

I glance over my shoulder to find him leaning there, just watching me. The smile on his face isn't one I've seen there before, like he knows something I don't, and it makes my pulse quicken in ways I wish it wouldn't.

What am I saying? Of course he knows something. He knows exactly what we're about to walk into. I've never met a celebrity in my life, and tonight I'll be surrounded by them. Exciting, but intimidating.

I take a deep breath. I've been in plenty of rooms I didn't belong in, and I've owned every single one of them. Wit, posture, the art of listening. I know the drill.

I don't wait for anyone to let me in. I wait to find the cracks in their confidence that I can use to my advantage. Being an outsider isn't a weakness; it's my superpower.

I finish my makeup, slide on the pair of pointed black stilettos Locke bought me, and give myself one last look in the mirror.

Wine-colored silk hugs my curves, with a halter neckline that plunges deep, meeting a fitted waist, and leaving my back exposed.

The fabric pools behind me in soft drapes. It looks elegant... until I move.

Then the twin slits up both thighs flash skin with every step, leaving little to be imagined. It has a classy sexiness, and I'm hoping it's tempting enough to catch the eye of a certain actor.

I stride toward the doorway where Locke still leans, blocking the exit. "You're just jealous that I look better than you. Don't worry, I won't steal the spotlight *too much*."

Locke lets out a bark of a laugh. "Let's hope you don't cause too much of a stir." His eyes sweep down my body and back up again as he says it, heat in every inch of his gaze.

I grin up at him. "Looks like it might be too late."

I follow him out the door where a blacked-out SUV is already waiting for us. The windows are so dark there's absolutely no chance of anyone seeing us inside. I didn't know Locke had a driver, but I step inside and settle into the black leather seats, nonetheless.

We're mostly quiet in the car. My mind is too busy racing. It's like too many tabs are open in my brain. Thoughts keep swirling and crashing into each other until I can barely remember who I am or why I ever agreed to this.

We finally catch a glimpse of the venue ahead: an extravagant outdoor garden sprawling around a glittering reception hall.

A swarm of photographers out front crowds a small red carpet, cameras firing like machine guns. Even from here, the flashes are blinding. My eyes fly to Locke's. He's calm and steady, like this is just another Friday night.

He must catch the look of dread on my face because he whispers, "I thought you were ready to steal the spotlight."

But the focused look that follows tells me he already has a backup plan. He leans forward and mutters something to the driver. The car keeps rolling, bypassing the chaos.

I bite the inside of my lip to keep from asking where the hell we're going. This doesn't feel like the moment for questions.

The driver takes us around the block, to the opposite side of the garden. Locke murmurs that someone will open a service door and, sure enough, we hop out of the car and slip into the reception hall unseen.

Relief washes over me as soon as we're inside. He notices, guiding me forward with a hand at the small of my back. The gesture is protective, not romantic, but I still feel a spark where his skin grazes mine.

The reception hall is mostly empty. Tables are still being set, and a lone microphone waits on stage. Soon there will be speeches and champagne toasts, but for now, we move quickly, blending with the trickle of service workers.

The sight before me and the sweet perfume of flowers steal my breath when we exit the building and step into the garden. Winding pathways are lined with flowers in varying shades of pink, purple, and blue.

String lights hang between the trees scattered over the grounds, and sitting areas consisting of vintage couches and coffee tables holding appetizers are placed in small grassy nooks. It's breathtaking and not at all what I expected.

I'd expected something flashy, loud, and overstimulating. Not this serene and low-key vibe. I'd also expected crowds, but we're early, and only a few other guests hover near the bar.

Locke orders us a round of drinks, and by the time he returns to the small coffee table flanked by two surprisingly comfortable chairs I've chosen, the crowd has swelled.

Celebrities flood in from the red-carpet entrance we managed to avoid. Actors, models, musicians. Some I recognize; some I don't. No one noteworthy, at least not to me.

Then, I feel it. There's a shift in the air, like all the oxygen is being sucked out of the room. And I see her step in: Sienna Vale.

The face of beauty. An untouchable goddess. The woman every girl wants to be. Her image has covered magazines, perfume campaigns, and lingerie ads for as long as I can remember.

Yet here she is, glittering in champagne sequins with a blush-pink faux fur shrug slung low around her shoulders. A walking disco ball who looks perfectly at home, thriving in this space. I try to rip my gaze away, but my eyes refuse to listen.

As she settles in at a table, her eyes sweep the crowd. She notices

Locke first, and her face lights up with recognition. When she notices me next to him, her eyes narrow in assessment, and she immediately stands again. A venomous smile curves the corners of her mouth as she strolls in our direction.

I know that smile. It's the same one I wear when I've chosen my mark. *Lucky us.*

Locke seems to have noticed, too, because he's gone completely still. I've never seen him like this. Not speaking, not smirking, not even pretending at control. If he's still breathing, I can't tell.

The man who commands every room he walks into is frozen solid. There must be a history here, and whatever happened between them is clearly something even I can't comprehend. I brace myself as she closes the distance.

"Locke!" she croons, wrapping her arms around him in a hug that looks staged for cameras that aren't even here. Clearly, this is her performance, and we're just the supporting actors.

"Sienna," Locke mutters in a tone full of grit and disdain. Letting her and me both know exactly how he feels about seeing her tonight.

She ignores it, taking a step back to brush away a strand of hair that has fallen in front of his face. "It's been so long; you look even more handsome than the last time I saw you." Her gaze snaps to me as she says it. I fight the urge to roll my eyes, but keep my mouth shut.

Locke backs away to escape her grip. His lips twitch, and a spark of amusement glints in his eyes as he pulls me in closer. "This is Arden. My date."

I slide my arms around him and flash her a wicked smile. "Nice to meet you, Sienna. I'm a huge fan."

A look of surprise that quickly turns into irritation takes over her expression, but she recovers fast, bypassing me and turning that smile back on Locke. "I didn't realize you were bringing company."

"Funny," he shoots back, "I didn't realize you were still relevant enough to be here."

Sienna's eyes narrow, just a fraction. "Careful, Locke," she murmurs. "We both know how messy things can get when we argue."

I lean in closer to his chest, and his arm comes around me without hesitation. Sienna's smile tightens in a way that lets me know she isn't a fan.

The tension hangs between us, her eyes daring me to look away first. I won't. I've had too many run-ins with real-life monsters to let a washed-up mean girl have the upper hand.

Instead, I shift my hold on Locke so that we face each other. I reach up, my fingers tracing the exact line of his temple where her hand just was.

I don't just touch him; I purposely hook my finger under that same strand of hair she just tucked away and pull it back down. I watch it fall across his forehead, messy and effortless, exactly the way he usually wears it.

Those golden whiskey eyes meet mine, and his breath hitches, a low, rough sound that has nothing to do with the woman standing two feet away. I keep my hand there, my thumb tracing the edge of his cheekbone as I finally turn my head to look at her.

"I don't know," I say, my voice dripping with feigned innocence as I admire my work. "I think he looks much better when he isn't so polished. It's a bit more authentic, don't you think, Sienna?"

The silence that follows is deafening. Sienna's face goes from pale and flawless to blotchy, insulted red. She looks like she wants to reach out and strangle me. Locke's hand settles firmly on my waist, pulling me flush against his side, claiming me without saying a word.

Sienna scoffs, and her nostrils flare. A sharp intake of breath is the only thing keeping her from making a scene. Without another word, her heels echo a sharp clicking sound against the walkway as she retreats into the crowd.

I wait until she's out of earshot before I finally let go of him, though I don't move out of his space. His expression is full of shock, a dark sort of amusement, and something else... something raw, almost primal.

"So..." I murmur, "you dated Sienna Vale?" My heart hammers in my chest from the rush of watching her perfect mask crumble, and the heat of his hand still resting comfortably on my waist.

His jaw flexes, disgust dripping from his voice as he says, "Honestly? It's something I try to forget."

I'm still perplexed, but grinning when movement near the entrance catches my eye, and everything inside me goes still. A man just walked in fashionably late.

He's taller than I expected, maybe six-foot-two, with a perfect tan and Hollywood smile that probably cost more than my car. He pretends not to notice that all eyes are on him as he adjusts his pristine navy suit jacket and runs a hand over his slicked-back blonde hair. But it's the eyes that get me. They're bored, predatory, scanning the crowd like everyone here is beneath him, no matter who they are.

"Well, well," I breathe as Locke straightens beside me. "It's him."

He nods once. "I know he looks harmless, all charm and practiced smiles, but don't underestimate him."

"I won't." I down what's left in my glass, setting it on a nearby table as I step toward the crowd. "But he's about to underestimate me."

Chapter 18
LOCKE

The women I prefer are never boring. I guess that's my type. Sienna came in and stirred things up, as usual. But she wildly underestimated her opponent this time. Arden proved it even further when she noticed Luke Holloway walk in.

She didn't hesitate, just slipped into the crowd, with a sly smile and those sharp eyes, moving toward him like a lioness stalking her prey. I should have known she wouldn't wait for me to be ready or give her the go-ahead. Of course she'd go straight for the kill.

I could have used a moment to recover from all the bullshit seeing Sienna stirred up in me, but here we are.

I force myself to stay calm on the surface, even though I'm already unraveling inside. I watch as she "accidentally" trips, spilling a fresh drink on his perfectly tailored suit. His eyes turn from annoyance to predatory lust as soon as they land on her face.

Within minutes, they're laughing as if they've known each other for years. She touches his arm, leans in, and whispers something in his ear. He gives her a wicked smirk in return.

I watch as he places his hand on the small of her back as they continue their conversation. The same way I did as we walked in. That gesture alone sends fire raging through my veins. Then, his eyes drag down her body, and I want to break something. Preferably his face.

I can't do this again. Watching them flirting from across the garden, being powerless to stop him from saying, or doing, whatever he wants to her. It's giving me a sick sense of déjà vu that makes my stomach churn.

Before, it was Sienna; I watched him use the same practiced charm to dismantle what we had, piece by piece, until she was a shell of the woman I once knew and wanted nothing to do with 'someone like me' any longer. Those words were a turning point. In that moment, I decided never to let another woman make me feel like who I was, at my core, was something to be hidden.

I also haven't had a serious relationship since.

It seems that Luke has a twisted instinct for finding a woman who catches my eye and making her his prize. He doesn't even need to know her name to know he wants to take her from me. It's a calculated game where he doesn't just win; he ensures I lose. That's how I know this plan, this job I've given her, will work.

Keep it together, Locke. Don't make headlines tonight.

But my feet are already moving. I can't let her stay near him for another second. I snatch two drinks from a passing server, not even caring what's in them, and cut across the garden. My heart is a sledgehammer against my ribs as I close the distance.

As I come up behind them, Luke grins down at her, absolutely shameless. "You're easily the most captivating person here. You should join me at the after-party. My place. It's going all night."

Arden's lips curve, sweet as poison. "Tempting, but I don't usually follow strange men home."

He leans closer; his voice is so low I have to concentrate to hear it over the rest of the crowd. "Trust me, sweetheart. You won't regret it."

Before Arden can reply, I step in. "She's busy."

Luke's eyes dart up, irritation flashing before it melts into a satisfied smirk. "Locke, it's been a while." His gaze drifts between us. "Didn't know you'd brought a date. Not really your style, is it?"

I bare my teeth in something that hardly feels like a smile. "I guess tonight is full of surprises."

I glance over, and Arden's glare is sharp enough to kill.

Luke chuckles, slick and dismissive. "I guess so."

His eyes flick to her again, gauging her reaction, and he smiles to himself. "Well, when he's done playing bodyguard, Arden, call me. I'll be waiting." He winks at her, then slithers back into the crowd like the snake he is. Walking past everyone else as if they don't even exist.

The second he's out of sight, Arden whirls on me, eyes blazing. "What the fuck!" she hisses, barely keeping her voice down.

"I couldn't stand the way he was looking at you. Undressing you with his eyes like you were just a piece of meat."

"*Díos mio*, Locke." She sighs, pinching the bridge of her nose. "You let that moment with Sienna get to your head, didn't you? We aren't together, and just because I'm working for you doesn't mean you own me. I was just playing their little games!"

Her voice dips lower at the end of that sentence, like she's worried someone might overhear.

"That's why I'm here, isn't it? To get close to him?"

She's right. I told her to do this, and to gain his trust.

Maybe I should have mentioned that *he's* not the only man I was hoping she'd get close to.

I cut that thought short before I let my imagination go too far. This whole situation is getting messier by the minute. I'm not sure she wants to be standing next to me, let alone 'getting close' to me, right now. I'm not sure I should want that either. Could it ever really work?

"You're right. I'm sorry," I say, shaking my head. "I just know what he's capable of, and I don't want to see you get hurt."

Her laugh comes out bitter. "I can take care of myself. Trust me. I've been doing it for a long time, and I've dealt with guys a hell of a lot scarier than that asshole."

Even though I know she's still underestimating what Luke is capable of, I believe her. The way she says it makes me wonder exactly how much of her past I don't know. How much she'll never tell me.

"I get it. I won't intrude again. You're not going anywhere near his place, though. I know what happens at those parties, and I won't let you walk into that house of horrors."

"You don't get to tell me what I will and will not do!" she hisses, attempting to shove me away. It's a cute effort, but I take hold of her arm instantly, pulling her in close.

"Don't I?" I murmur, leaning in. "You're my employee. You said it yourself."

"Employee, not property," she shoots back, baring her teeth. "What I do off the clock is none of your concern."

Her defiance is intoxicating, a wildfire I have no business trying to tame. But a shadow in my peripheral vision reminds me we aren't alone, and Luke isn't the only one that might be watching. I know better than anyone that nothing good comes from making a scene at an event like this.

"Hate to break it to you, but you're never off the clock with me," I mutter. "You'd do well to remember exactly what's at stake." I finally release my hold on her arm, and my hand feels noticeably colder the moment we break contact.

She avoids my gaze as she adjusts her dress and mutters something about needing the restroom. She's still playing her role, but I'm reeling.

Watching her leave, I realize with a sinking gut feeling that I'm not just worried about Luke taking her in a romantic sense. I'm worried about what might happen when I can't be there to protect her and what he might try to take when he gets her alone.

When she returns, we both stay quiet. I know she's upset about my interference, and I won't push her any further.

Sitting down for dinner is a special kind of torture; her assigned seat is directly next to mine, while four other guests sit around the table with us. None of whom I know on a personal level.

The table feels much smaller than it looks. Each tiny movement we make is met with the subtle pressure of her shoulder or elbow brushing against mine. That, paired with the rhythmic clinking of silverware on porcelain, the heavy scent of roasted meat and red wine, and the loud, forced chatter in the confined space, is almost unbearable. I'm being pushed to my limit, and I haven't even reached for my fork.

In the background, the director of the foundation speaks. His voice drones on, a dull and bleak soundtrack to my growing exasperation. He says something about their "mission and vision" that I'm only half paying attention to.

Instead, I'm captivated by the way the chandelier light glints off Arden's necklace as she eats. Every time she tilts her head, the diamonds catch the light. It's a subtle and cruel reminder of how brightly she truly shines and makes me wonder how many other eyes in this room might notice that same sparkle.

Each speech is harder to get through than the last. Although she still hasn't spoken, Arden's presence is heavy, and the familiar tension around us is becoming suffocating. She turns slightly to sip her water, and her arm grazing mine sends a shock shooting up my spine.

"You look like you're about to break something," she whispers. The words are so hushed they're almost lost in the applause for a local donor. She doesn't look at me, just keeps her eyes fixed on the stage with a polite smile plastered to her face.

"I'm fine," I mutter back, but my jaw is so tight it aches.

"You're brooding, Locke. It'd be clear from the back of the room." She finally cuts a glance toward me, her eyes flashing with a mix of continued defiance and concern. "Let it go."

I don't answer. She turns her attention back to the stage, leaving me to simmer in silence again.

When it's finally my turn to speak, the stage actually feels like an escape. I step toward the podium, relishing the cool, floral-scented air. It's a relief from the heat of her presence beside me.

I stare out at the sea of faces, delivering the same polished speech I've given a dozen times before. I talk about the kind of legacy I want to leave and responsibility to the community. My voice comes out smooth, even as my eyes instinctively scan the crowd for Luke's shark-like grin.

I find him near the bar, watching not the stage, but the table I just left. Watching Arden.

The polite applause barely registers as I make my way back to my seat. I feel detached, like a ghost in my own body. Hollow and entirely too focused on the woman sitting just inches away.

The rest of the night is a blur of handshakes and thank-yous. Arden acts the part of the perfect date, doling out polite smiles and compliments.

She goes silent again on the trip home, but I can feel her watching me. The car is a dark, quiet sanctuary after the sensory overload of the gala. The streetlights flicker across her face in rhythmic pulses of color and shadow. I look over, and her eyes meet mine. She doesn't look angry anymore, just tired. She gives me a faint, uncertain smile, like she's trying to bridge the gap I forced between us earlier.

I nod and pat the leather seat, motioning for her to scoot into the space beside me. She hesitates for a heartbeat before sliding over. I wrap my arm around her shoulders, pulling her firmly against my side. She rests her head on my chest, her hair smelling like the night air and the expensive perfume she wore for another man's benefit. We stay like that for the rest of the drive, the silence finally softening.

I don't understand this girl, not even close. But as I tighten my grip on her shoulder, I realize I'm starting to care for her a little too much.

Chapter 19

ARDEN

It's almost 11 when we walk through the door to Locke's mansion. My feet ache from the ridiculous heels, my head buzzes from too much champagne, and my skin is drenched in the scent of perfume that isn't mine.

The events of the last few hours have left me feeling drained, both mentally and physically. I should sleep. I should lock the door and let the world go dark. But Locke's voice is a splinter in my mind, incessant and impossible to ignore. *'You're not going anywhere near his place.'*

Honestly, who is he to tell me I can't go?

'You're never off the clock with me.' We'll see about that.

Locke disappears down the maze of hallways leading toward his room, distracted by an oddly-timed phone call, and the silence in this house instantly feels suffocating. I stand there, my hand hovering over the bedroom doorknob, my vision blurring with exhaustion. Every muscle in my body is screaming for the mattress, or a hot bath, but my pulse is doing something else. Racing with frantic, and quite possibly stupid, curiosity.

I don't give myself time to change my mind. I peel off the gown with shaking hands, and slide into an outfit that feels more like a weapon: my favorite pair of faded ripped jeans and a black tank top.

My usual boots with chunky heels finish the look, and I'm out the back door in a matter of minutes.

My pulse hammers in my chest as I sneak past the pool. Not from fear, but excitement... pure adrenaline. Every shadow feels like it's watching, every step dares him to catch me. I inspect the perimeter of the house as I sneak past. Are there cameras? Probably. Do I care? Not even a little.

I tell myself it's just curiosity, and that I'll only peek in. I just need to know what kind of man I'm really up against. A few minutes. Pure research.

My boots hit the pavement, one after another, until I'm sliding into the backseat of a rideshare. The city blurs by, and with every flashing light, reality sets in — there's absolutely no turning back now.

The car crunches up the gravel drive of Luke's sprawling mansion, stopping to let me out before continuing back down to the main road. The house is dark, but bursts of color flash in the windows. Red, violet, gold, blue, like the house itself is breathing in time with the bass I can hear from outside the front door.

I don't bother knocking, just push the door open and step over the threshold. To my surprise, there are two security guards dressed in black suits flanking the entrance. The top halves of their faces are hidden behind ornate gold domino masks.

"Phone," one of them says, shoving a small plastic bin in my direction.

"Phone?" I echo. My voice is a combination of shock and bewilderment.

The guard on my opposite side leans in and whispers, "Put your phone in the basket."

A giant knot instantly forms in my stomach. Not just because they want my phone, but also because what he said came dangerously close to, "It puts the phone in the basket." Not a great vibe.

With a shaky breath, I ignore the sinking feeling and reach into the back pocket of my jeans. I glance down before handing the phone over, and my eyes snag on the screen. It's flooded with notifications: calls, text messages, even a video call — all from Locke. *I guess he's their problem now.*

The chaos inside the house is all-consuming, beckoning me in. The air is hot and thick with the scent of perfume and sweat and something else... metallic. I scan the room, trying to orient myself or find a familiar face, which seems to pose a problem because every headline I've ever read is staring back at me. Actors, models, pro athletes... they're all here.

Every one of them wears a smile that doesn't quite reach their glassy eyes, and their movements are loose in a way that sends prickles down my spine. Whatever's in the punch, I'm staying far away from it.

I inch forward, circling the perimeter of the room, eyes fighting to focus with each flash of light. I'm not sure if my head is spinning from the aftereffects of the alcohol I drank earlier or the music I can barely hear myself think over.

Female servers weave through the crowd in matching black silk slips that cling to their skin and look far too short to be uniforms. The same ornate gold masks the security guards wore obscure their faces, too. Other girls, dressed the same, stand scattered in corners, completely silent, their gazes fixed on nothing. Like they're decorations, rather than guests.

A tall, muscular man reaches out as he passes one of them. He casually runs his hand up the length of her thigh, lifting the dress slightly to reveal a barely-there lace thong underneath. His gaze roams over every inch of her body as he licks his lips. She doesn't react to any of it.

What the fuck is this?

My heart beats like a war drum in my chest, and I feel like I might be sick. I turn my head, desperately needing a distraction.

Then, my gaze lands on a long table in the center of the room. Not a normal table, more like an elevated trough. My stomach drops as soon as I realize what's in it.

There's a female body stretched out under spotlights. Her skin is deathly pale, naked limbs arranged just so and partially submerged in viscous red liquid. No, that's not... It can't be... am I hallucinating?

My throat begins to close as I realize people are standing around it... staring... eating?

As I inch closer, faces come into view. A huddle of women, all tall and unnaturally thin, licking their lips that are stained deep red. I overhear a familiar voice and turn to see none other than Sienna Vale excitedly chattering to the woman beside her. "Try the blood; it's delicious!"

What the fuck. What the fuck. What the fuck.

As I close in on the table, I catch bits and pieces of other conversations.

"It's so realistic!"

"It's pure art."

"I wonder what's on the inside."

As I approach the edge of the table, I notice one of Sienna's friends is holding up a large kitchen knife. She plunges the blade into the woman's thigh before I can even think about what's happening. My eyes go wide in pure horror. I clamp both hands over my mouth to keep myself from screaming.

She pulls the knife away, blood-red liquid filling the space where the chunk of flesh used to be. But it's not flesh on her plate. It's... chocolate cake?

The crowd is giggling now, dipping fingers into the pool of thick red liquid and licking them off. Plunging forks and spoons directly into the perfectly glazed frosting that looks so much like actual skin.

They act like it's a joke, but every instinct in me screams that there's something deeper behind it. I want to run, duck out before anyone recognizes me, especially Sienna, but I feel a hand on my shoulder before I can even move.

Then a slick, familiar voice is in my ear. "Isn't it beautiful?" Luke murmurs. His voice is smooth as silk, completely unbothered by the events unfolding around him. "It was Sienna's idea."

I glance back toward the group of women surrounding the supermodel, then at him. "Are you two together now?"

He gives me a smirk that tells me he's flattered by the question. "I guess you could say that... although we have more of an open relationship."

"I see," I reply, looking up at him through my lashes.

His hand still rests on my shoulder, and he gives me an assessing look, like he's trying to solve a puzzle. "I'm surprised you came. Didn't know Locke had a new lady."

I huff out a single breath. "We're not a couple. It was just one date."

He raises his eyebrows. "Oh, in that case, come see what's out back. That's where the real fun is."

Just then, a shadow falls over us and a hand clamps down over Luke's on my shoulder. The pressure is firm enough that it actually hurts.

"Actually, we were just heading home," a deep, possessive voice cuts in. Locke.

I jump at the sudden intrusion, and spin to see his dark eyes glaring at Luke. Luke still seems completely unfazed as a slow grin spreads across his face.

"Locke!" I say, trying not to sound too relieved.

Luke slides his hand from beneath Locke's, though his smirk remains. "Just showing your date what real fun is. I'm sure this," he says, gesturing to the surrounding chaos, "is a bit loud for your tastes, Locke. But some women actually prefer a little noise to the polite silence you offer."

Locke's eyes narrow. "She's with me. That's all that matters."

"Right, right," Luke says, chuckling.

He leans in toward me, ignoring the growing tension. "Just know the offer still stands. Something tells me you prefer some excitement to being leashed."

Locke's jaw tightens, and I make sure I'm positioned between them.

I turn to Luke again. "If I were you, I wouldn't underestimate how much I might like a good leash." I give him a playful wink. Then, turning to Locke, "Care to walk me out?"

Locke doesn't say a word, but his grip on my hand is firm as he leads me away, his watchful presence a solid wall between me and Luke.

My pulse pounds so hard I'm sure he can feel it through my skin. I give him a weak smile as we head towards the door. He doesn't smile back.

Before we can make it out, two burly men wearing the same suits and ornate gold masks as the security guards from earlier cut in front of us. They're each gripping an arm of a girl who can't be a day over 20.

She's frantic, writhing and screaming. As they drag her toward the door, I glimpse her face. The fight left her cheeks flushed, and trails of mascara smudged down them.

It feels as if the room is spinning. Where did they even bring her from? She's not wearing a black slip or gold mask like the servers, so she must be a guest.

I turn toward Locke. His expression mirrors the same concern and confusion I'm feeling. He reaches into his suit jacket and pulls out a small black rectangle. "I'll go check on her; you go outside," he says as he presses my phone into my palm. He's chasing after the guards before I can ask how he got it.

The brisk night air slams into me like a slap to the face. I welcome the sensation, taking a deep breath in. I tilt my head back, searching for stars that aren't there. Exhaling a cloud of silver breath, I square my shoulders, lowering my chin again as the world rushes back to meet me. I'm just glad to finally be out of that house.

That's when I spot him. Nate. He leans casually against his motorcycle at the edge of the drive, helmet on the seat, as smoke curls from a cigarette between his gloved fingers.

He looks me over once, a faint smirk tugging at his mouth, like he already knows exactly what I've just witnessed, what happened with Locke, and thinks I deserved all of it. "I'm ready to take you home," he calls out to me, "unless you want to be the next one on the table." He chuckles at that remark. The smug bastard.

I don't respond. My throat is tight. I can't get any words out past the shock of what I just saw and the very high chance that there were even more horrors to be discovered. Not to mention, I still have no idea what Locke has to say about all this.

I just tug on the helmet, climb on the bike, and exhale a sigh of relief as the engine's roar drowns out the sound of twisted laughter still spilling from Luke's open windows.

The city lights blend in streaks of red and gold as we cut through the night. I can finally let myself breathe as Nate puts more and more distance between us and the party. At a stop, he leans back just enough for his words to carry over the engine.

"Was the party worth the lecture you'll be getting from my brother?"

"I don't even understand how parties like that exist," I say flatly, trying and failing to erase the images from my mind.

Nate chuckles, but it's not lighthearted. It's dark. Like he knows. "Locke hired you for your skills. Clearly, not your common sense."

"What do you mean by that?" I reply, not entirely sure I'm hiding the embarrassment in my voice.

"It just might do you some good to listen to my brother for once."

I arch a brow. "Oh, you mean just let him control everything I do? Because the jail threats aren't enough?"

Nate just shrugs. "You brought this on yourself, girl. All the lying and stealing has finally caught up with you."

I don't reply. I know what he's saying is the truth; I just don't think I'm ready to face it.

Nate keeps quiet for the rest of the ride home. It's only when he's parked his motorcycle at the top of Locke's gravel driveway that he speaks again.

"Listen. Do your job. Stop acting like you have something to prove." He pauses to light another cigarette. I can't help but shake my head. *These men and their smoking habits.*

"Most importantly, get to know him. You might be surprised at how much the two of you actually have in common."

My brow furrows at him. "How could you possibly know what we have in common?"

He shrugs. "You both give off the same 'lone wolf, can't trust anyone but myself' vibe. You must have *something* in common."

I can't stop the laughter that bubbles up in my chest.

Nate's phone lets out a loud *ding* that echoes through the night's calm air. He glances at it, then back up at me.

"Locke is on his way. He said you should pack a bag; you have a flight in an hour."

Chapter 20

ARDEN

I'm basking in the small mercy of a hot shower when Locke walks through the door. I hear him call out for me as I turn the water off and wrap a plush white towel around my body.

My overstuffed duffel bag is already packed and waiting on the bed. Without any details about the trip, I packed everything that fit.

I throw on my most comfortable sweatpants and hoodie. I have no idea how long this flight will be, and wherever we're going, I want to be comfortable.

Locke's voice echoes down the hallway as he makes his way to my room. "Arden?"

"I'm almost ready!" I call back.

"Are you dressed?" is all he says before turning the handle and opening the door.

I level him with a flat stare as he walks in and makes himself comfortable on the bed, resting his elbows on his knees.

"Well, I'm dressed. Why do I get the feeling that you were hoping I wasn't?"

He doesn't laugh or smirk. The corners of his lips don't even twitch. He's just looking at me with that unreadable expression I've become all too familiar with. I just wait, taking the moment to towel dry my hair.

"Never do that to me again."

I blink at him. "To you?"

"Yes, *to me*. Do you even realize what that's like? To watch you sneak away? Knowing you're going exactly where I told you not to, just to spite me?"

He's completely serious. This doesn't seem like just a control issue. He's actually hurt?

"I don't think you understand what this place is actually like. You could have gotten into some deep shit."

"I don't think I understood how *deranged* it actually is. But trust me, after the glimpse I got tonight, I fully believe you."

I walk over to the bed, my footsteps soft against the carpet, and stop at the foot. I pretend I want to add my makeup bag to the practically overflowing duffel, the zipper straining as I close it back up. But truly, I just want to feel his warmth near me.

"I'm just glad you're okay," he mutters.

"Thanks for coming to get me." I stare down at him. The way he's hunched over. Elbows resting on his knees, hands clasped together, eyes glued to the floor. He looks exhausted.

He turns his head, and his gaze lifts to mine. "What else would I have done?"

I just stare. "You could have... not come." I shrug. "No one's ever come to save me before," I admit, batting my eyelashes playfully, trying to make light of it. But it's the honest truth.

His lips finally twitch; there's a hint of a smile there now. Just enough to let me know he's no longer angry.

He stands, grabbing my bag and throwing the long strap over his shoulder. "We should go. It's a long flight to Italy, and we're on a rigid timeline."

Italy. I don't even have a passport in my bag, but somehow Locke makes it sound inevitable. Like I was always going, whether I wanted to or not. I swallow the hundred questions fighting their way up my throat and give him a smile instead.

Despite the shock, Italy sounds amazing. I'll trust that he has the details worked out.

Minutes later, I'm being shoved into a car. It's just after 2 a.m., and I desperately want to be sleeping. Instead, we're being driven to the airport in another blacked-out SUV.

Of course we don't pull up at a normal airport. Why would we? We arrive at a sleek building with mirrored windows that looks more like a private club than anything air-travel related. No signs. No lines. Just a guy in a suit who quickly opens the door and helps me out of the car. Locke doesn't say a word as he exits behind me.

The same guy grabs our bags as Locke guides me through the sleek sliding doors with his hand on the small of my back. He's been doing that a lot.

I'm still processing the fact that I'm about to hop on a plane with a man I was shamelessly flirting with in front of his supermodel ex-girlfriend a few hours ago, who also just helped me escape a party straight out of hell.

Someone tell me how this became my Friday night?

The inside of the terminal, if you can even call it that, has velvet chairs, a small coffee bar, and someone handing me a flute of champagne as I walk in. I still can't get used to these minor details that are somehow normal in this world.

Before I can get comfortable, or make a cup of coffee, we're already being ushered onto the tarmac. At least the plane looks normal from the outside. Smaller than other planes I've been on, but normal. I walk up the small set of stairs, Locke following behind me, and step in.

I lied. This is anything but normal.

I'm met with a view of wide, cream-colored leather seats, two facing each other on each side of the aisle. There's a small sitting area with a couch lining the wall and a TV stand across from it. Wood panels conceal another space in the back, but I'm too stunned to wonder what might be behind them.

I sink into one of the plush seats; it's far more comfortable than any other plane seat I've ever been in, and there's plenty of room to stretch my legs.

Locke chooses the seat directly across from me. I'm still holding my champagne as a woman in a fitted navy uniform sets a bottle of whiskey and two glasses on the ledge next to him. She mutters something about takeoff and mentions the length of our flight: eleven hours.

Eleven hours in the sky. With him. With my own thoughts. I'm not sure which is worse.

"Why, exactly, are we suddenly on a plane to Italy?" The words spill out before I have a chance to ponder why he might be keeping that information from me.

His lips spread in a wide grin. "It's a surprise."

"A surprise? For me?" I narrow my eyes at him. "I don't like surprises. Can't you just tell me?"

He chuckles, shaking his head slightly and sipping his fresh glass of whiskey. "Nope, you'll just have to wait."

I cross my arms, pouting for a moment before leaning back and downing what's left of my champagne. Then, I close my eyes, hoping I'll finally be able to get some sleep after the long night we've had.

They don't stay closed long before I hear his familiar voice.

"Another?" My eyes snap open, and I see Locke standing right in front of me.

"Are you trying to get me drunk already?" I snap back.

He shrugs. "Just trying to make this flight tolerable."

"For you or for me?"

He doesn't answer, but his mouth twitches like he's amused by the question.

"I don't want to get drunk; I just want to sleep," I add.

He says nothing in return. Instead, he drops into a crouch, his shoulder brushing my knee as he unlatches a hidden compartment at the base of my seat.

He pulls out a small, plush blanket, shaking it open in front of him. The movement makes me flinch. It's a small reaction, but he notices and pauses.

I spent years tucking blankets around a woman who didn't even seem to feel them, checking for a pulse that eventually wasn't there. I don't need his version of care. I don't want anybody looking after me.

Still, as he leans in to drape the cashmere over my lap, his smoky, woodsy scent hits me. Suddenly, I forget I don't want this. I forget how to breathe.

"Get comfortable," he mutters, the words sharp in the quiet space, but he doesn't move. He stays right in front of me, waiting, his gaze unwavering.

I don't move, just mutter a quiet "thanks" before closing my eyes again.

Then, he slowly picks up his glass and relaxes back into his own seat.

Chapter 21

LOCKE

It's been over an hour, and neither of us has slept. We haven't said a single word to each other either, but we don't need to.

Every second on this plane tightens the tension between us. I should say something, break the silence, maybe tell her what surprise is waiting for us in Italy. But I can't rip my eyes away from the curve of her perfect lips.

The events of the night play on a loop in my head. Nate dropping her off at my door, Luke's party, whatever that moment was in front of Sienna. Any of those should have shaken her up. Instead, she's sitting across from me with her head tilted back and eyes closed. Pretending to sleep again, or trying to.

Her eyelashes flutter, and she crosses her legs slowly. Can she sense that I'm watching?

"Are you always this fun on international flights?" I ask. A playful overtone lacing the words.

She doesn't move right away, but it's like a challenge when she fully opens her eyes. "Are you always this annoying at 3 a.m.?" she shoots back, with fire in her eyes and a raspy voice from the half-sleep.

There she is.

I find myself huffing a quiet laugh; the sound vibrating in the small space between us.

"What's so funny?" she demands, her eyes narrowing as she shifts in her seat.

"Oh, nothing," I murmur, ice clinking against the glass as I pour another whiskey. "I was just thinking about the look on Sienna's face earlier. I don't think I've ever seen anyone leave her that speechless."

Her expression falters for a split second, her gaze dropping to my mouth before snapping back to my eyes. "I was just playing her game."

"Playing?" I arch a brow, my voice dropping to a low rumble. "You were marking your territory, and we both know it."

That gets to her, at least a little. She doesn't admit it, but she doesn't deny it, either. She hesitates for a second too long before responding.

"Don't flatter yourself, Locke," she whispers, though her pulse is visibly thrumming at the base of her throat. "I just wasn't about to let a woman like that think she had the upper hand."

My gaze drops, snagging on the curve of her lips again. I can practically feel the heat coming off her.

"And you think you have it?" I murmur, my voice dropping lower. "The upper hand?"

Before she can answer, I reach for the bottle again, the amber liquid catching the dim cabin lighting as I pour a second glass. I hold it out to her, forcing her to lean into my space to take it. She takes the glass and grabs the bottle with her other hand, placing it on the ledge next to her seat.

I watch her lips part, just a fraction, like she's caught between a retort and a confession. We lock eyes, and her gaze burns hotter; it almost reminds me of the night we met. For a second, part of me wonders if she'll close the last few inches between us and straddle me right here.

But she doesn't.

Instead, those perfect lips close around the glass, and the whiskey disappears in one swift motion. She doesn't look away. "You're playing a dangerous game, Locke," she says, her voice regaining that sharp, untouchable edge.

"Is that a warning?" I murmur, leaning across the aisle until I'm inches from her. "Because I've never been one to play it safe."

She lets out a dry, breathless laugh. "It's an observation. You like the idea of me. The mystery. But you'd have no idea what to do with the reality once you actually have it."

"Then give it to me," I challenge, my voice dropping to a rough rumble that vibrates in my chest. "Let's find out exactly how much reality I can handle."

I stand, desperately needing to move, and when I step in her direction, I ensure it's with intention. I lean over her to reclaim the bottle from the ledge, and the air between us practically sparks.

She doesn't flinch, doesn't pull back. Instead, she tilts her chin up, her gaze slowly raking over me with an intensity that makes my blood turn to fire.

"No, Locke," she whispers, the corner of her mouth twitching into a ghost of a smile. "I think you should go to sleep."

The words are a dismissal, but the look in her eyes is a dare. It's a punch straight to the gut. She's calling my bluff, telling me to back off because she knows exactly how close I am to cracking.

A slow, sharp smile of my own takes shape. Not because I'm happy, but because the gloves are officially off. She knows exactly what she's doing, and she's enjoying every second of watching me struggle.

"Fine," I say, my hand tightening around my glass.

I take a final, heavy pour of whiskey, the scent of her jasmine perfume and the sharp sting of the alcohol blurring into one intoxicating haze.

She closes her eyes, leaning her head back against the seat as if the conversation is over. But the quickened rise and fall of her chest give her away. She isn't sleeping. She's waiting.

I drop back into my seat across from her, my heart hammering a frenzied rhythm I can't control. I know one thing for sure: I won't be sleeping one goddamn minute of this flight.

I don't sleep.

I don't even close my eyes.

I just sit, watching her. The way her pulse flutters in her throat. The way her lips part when she exhales. She's trying to pretend she's calm, but I can feel her tension. I can almost taste it.

She has no idea what she's done to me. I swore I'd never let another woman get this close. Never give Luke another target to aim at. It's too late now; I'm already past the point of no return.

When we step off this plane and she tries to pretend none of this ever happened, I already know I'll touch her again.

Not because I want to.

Because I need to.

Because she's mine, whether or not she wants to admit it yet.

Chapter 22
LOCKE

We land in Verona around 10 p.m. Street lamps spill pools of golden light onto the cobblestones, and the rhythmic clicking of her boots echoes through the cool night air as we head toward the car. Every step she takes draws my attention like a magnet I can't pull away from.

She says nothing. Just slips into the back seat, legs crossed, eyes forward like I'm not even here. I slide in next to her, close enough to feel the heat radiating off her skin, but I keep my hands to myself — for now.

The driver is a shadow in the front seat, quiet and discreet. The silence inside the car rings even louder in my ears than the jet engines we just left behind.

Outside, Verona creeps past the windows in slow motion. Candlelight flickers on tables in crowded piazzas, where clusters of people linger over late dinners and last glasses of wine. Warmth glows from behind shuttered windows and spills over balconies heavy with flowers.

It's the kind of beauty that asks nothing of you, just exists to be admired. Arden tries to hide it, but I see that glimmer in her eyes. She can't get enough.

I'm not looking at any of it, not really.

I only see her.

I watch the way she bites the inside of her cheek, the tension in her shoulders, the flicker in her eyes she can't hide. She's trying not to betray herself, not to give anything away. But I can see the cracks forming in her armor.

The drive stretches on, agonizingly slow, until we finally roll to a stop in front of the villa. It's a weathered stone building, with a wrought-iron gate and candles flickering in the windows, casting jagged shadows across the ivy climbing its walls. It's the kind of place that would be soft and romantic if the air between us weren't already so charged it feels ready to explode.

She steps out first, and I follow immediately, close enough to catch the sway of her hair, the jasmine scent of her perfume rolling off her body. Every step she takes is mine to anticipate. Every glance she thinks she hides, I see.

It's almost laughable how she still carries herself with that untouchable poise, pretending she's in control when we both know the very air between us is a live wire.

The moment we're through the door, the energy shifts. There's no staff. No distractions. No aisle between us. Just stone walls, low lights, and the heavy silence of the villa.

"Arden." Her name is a low vibration in my throat. I don't hide the hunger anymore. The flight is over. The wait is, too.

She stops, her back to me for a heartbeat before she turns. Her voice is frayed, but she's still trying to hold the line. "We're finally here, Locke. Like I said... go to sleep. We both should."

She's trying to hide behind the same dismissal she used on the plane, but here, in the shadows of the villa, it sounds more like a challenge. She's not tired; she's vibrating with the same restless energy that's currently hollowing out my chest.

"That's not going to work this time," I murmur, closing in on her.

It only takes two steps, and I'm in her space, but she doesn't retreat. Her ocean-blue eyes stay glued to mine, and the flame I saw at 30,000 feet is now a blazing inferno.

I take another step, forcing her back until her spine meets the cool stone wall. I don't stop until my body forms a cage around her, arms on both sides of her head, and my hips pinning her in place.

I can feel her pulse skittering against my own. It beats at a frantic pace that tells me everything she isn't saying.

"Go to sleep, Locke," she whispers again, but the words lack conviction, dying in the inch of space between our lips.

"Come on, Arden. We both know that's not what you really want." I look down at her. There's nowhere left for her to run. I can feel the heat radiating off her, see the way her chest rises and falls in the same frantic rhythm I've been tracking for hours.

"If you really want me to stop, say it."

She doesn't.

Doesn't tell me to stop.

Doesn't tell me to keep going, either.

Just tilts her chin up, never breaking eye contact, like she's daring me to finish what I just started.

And I plan on it.

I crash into her like waves on the shore, merciless and claiming. Every nerve in my body screams to own her, to mark her, to devour her completely. I won't stop until every inch of her is mine. Her gasp rips through me and shreds any ounce of restraint I had left.

I can't touch her fast enough. One hand is tangled in her hair; the other is dragging down her spine, gripping her thigh. I can't choose. I won't. I want all of her, all at once. Every breath, every shiver, every inch of skin beneath my hands fuels a fire I can no longer contain.

I wrap my hands around the back of her thighs, lifting her without hesitation. A surprised shriek slips from her lips, adding more fuel to the fire raging inside me. She clamps her legs around me instinctively, pressing into me, and I don't even care where the bedroom is.

I sit her on the kitchen island, her breath ragged and uneven, as my hips slide between her legs. I can feel her trembling before me, the sensation pushing me further into this feral need.

My mouth finds her neck, and her pulse is wild as I drag my teeth over the sensitive skin. Her hoodie hits the floor, then her top. I don't know if I'm pulling them off or she is, but it doesn't matter. I just know I need her naked. Now.

I lift her slightly, tugging her sweats down to her ankles before yanking them off and tossing them on the kitchen floor. Every movement, every piece of fabric, is mine to command.

I slide her to the edge of the counter, slipping a hand between her thighs. A wicked smirk spreads across my face as I feel the dripping arousal there. "How long have you been this wet for me? Since the gala? On the plane?" She stays quiet, but the look in her eyes tells me everything I need to know. I've been right all along.

Not wasting another second, I drop to my knees, my mouth tracing a path from her calf to the soft skin on the inside of her thigh. She moans quietly as I tease the sensitive area with my teeth and tongue. I hover there, allowing more tension to build between us.

I feel her body tense beneath my hands.

Trying to stay quiet or trying not to let me see how badly she wants this. Still grasping for some form of control, like she's not already coming undone.

I slide my palms up the sides of her thighs and grip her hips tightly. Hard enough that she can't move much without my permission. A shudder runs down the length of her body. Exactly.

I lower my mouth, lips brushing so close to her center that I can feel her shaking. But I don't give her what she wants. Not yet. "You're still trying to hold it together, aren't you?"

She opens her mouth to reply, but the only thing that leaves it is a gasp as I bite down, hard, on the inside of her thigh, and she squirms on the counter's edge.

I rise slightly, sliding one hand up and wrapping it firmly around her throat. Not enough to affect her breathing, but enough to get her attention. "Relax," I whisper in her ear, "or I'll take even longer." She whimpers in response as I plant a soft kiss on her jaw.

Her body stills as she draws in a breath, shaky but deep, steadying herself.

"That's right," I murmur, "Don't fight it." I lower my mouth back to her skin, letting her feel every word. "You don't have to pretend anymore, Arden. I want you to feel everything. And I want to hear how much you love it."

Her breath hitches, a jagged sound that cuts through the silence.

"Yes," she whispers. The word sounds more like a prayer than a promise.

She leans back on her hands; her legs draped over my shoulders. This time, I don't tease. I dive in, my tongue flat against her entrance, gliding up to meet her clit. A moan slips from her lips, louder now. I take her clit in my mouth, and she grinds against me, chasing more. Her body already revealing the truth she's tried so hard to hide.

Her body is already begging for release. I can feel it in the way her hips twitch, the breath caught in her throat, how her legs start to tense and shake.

I pull back, and she responds with a strangled noise: half moan, half protest. I press a kiss right above where she wants me most and look up at her. "Not yet."

She's glaring down at me, her hair wildly framing her face. Chest rising and falling like she's about to explode. "Why?" she breathes.

I rise again, this time grabbing her wrists and pinning them in place. "Because you've been playing this game for almost two weeks," I growl, "no more lying, Arden. Not after the way you acted at the gala." I lean in until our breaths mingle. "I'm done watching you pretend. I've already admitted I'm weak for you. Now it's your turn."

"So, if you want to come, if you want me to take you right here, you're going to beg for it."

She pauses; a quiet sigh slips through her lips. Then she whispers, "I don't beg."

I feel another wicked grin stretch across my face. "I thought you'd say that," I say casually, my hand drifting slowly up her thigh. "But we have all night."

I kiss my way back down the length of her neck, lazily. I stop when I reach her breast and close my mouth around her peaking nipple, biting just enough to make her jolt.

She'll beg; she just doesn't know it yet.

"Fuck this," she grits out between clenched teeth. "You're a sadistic bastard." We've been at this for what feels like hours but could just as easily have been minutes.

I glance up at her. "What I said before still stands. If you want me to stop, just say it."

"Chinga tu madre," is all she offers in return.

Her breathing is ragged now. Her eyes stay closed as she lies across the island, a thin layer of sweat making her golden skin glisten in the candlelight's glow.

"Fuck, Arden. You can insult me all you want if it sounds like that."

My hand slides between her thighs again. I've lost count of how many times I've done this tonight. I tease two fingers around her entrance before slowly slipping them inside and curving them against her.

My tongue glides over the sensitive skin near her hipbone, and I feel her body arch. "You really are a stubborn little thing, aren't you?" I feel the corners of my mouth lift and twist into a feral grin.

I slowly taste her, sucking her clit into my mouth while my fingers slide in and out of her lazily. It doesn't take long before her hips are arching into me, chasing the very thing she still refuses to ask for.

I pull away. Standing over her for what feels like the hundredth time tonight, my finger traces the delicate curve of her jaw. My hand slides to her chin, turning her face to meet mine. "Open for me."

Surprisingly, she obeys, opening her mouth for me. Her blue eyes stay pinned to mine as I press my fingers, coated in the salt and heat of her own body, into it.

She seals her lips, and I feel the slide of her tongue as I pull my fingers back.

That single act is enough to push me over the edge. I groan as my cock strains against my zipper. But this isn't about me. It's always been about her.

"Just wanted you to know how delicious you are. I could stay here until sunrise."

She holds my gaze, one last flicker of defiance in her eyes before the fight drains out of her all at once.

Her head tilts back, exposing the line of her throat, and her lips part.

And then... soft, broken, and furious.

"Please," she breathes.

I pause, waiting for more.

"Please, what?" I ask.

She pushes herself up on her elbows; her knuckles white against the stone countertop as she anchors herself. Her chest heaves with a sharp inhale, her gaze searching mine with a desperation she can't deny.

"Please let me come, Locke."

My smile widens. "Anything for you, Arden. All you had to do was ask."

She lets out a groan. "You're insufferable!"

Then, her eyes flutter shut in a silent, heavy admission of defeat. I move one hand down to grip the soft heat of her thigh and drop my mouth back to where she's soaked and aching for me.

She moans as if I've shattered something deep inside of her as her body finally finds release. Her back arches against me, and her fingers tangle in my hair as her thighs tremble against my shoulders.

The sound of it, the raw, broken edges of her voice, feeds a hunger in me I didn't even know was there. A flush of heat spreads from the base of my throat, and my cock presses harder against my zipper. I ignore it, admiring her instead.

Exhaustion has finally won. As she lies across the island, a single tear escapes her eye, tracking a slow, silver line down her temple and disappearing into her hair. It's the first thing she hasn't tried to hide from me. The mask hasn't just slipped; it's shattered.

Seeing her like this, stripped of every defense, I realize the only thing left to do is protect what's left. Without a word, I step closer, closing the distance she's kept between us for weeks. I reach for her, sliding my hands beneath her knees and shoulders, and scoop her into my arms.

As I carry her down the dimly lit hallway, the only sound is the rhythmic, heavy thud of my shoes against the wood and her soft, shallow breath against my neck. She feels fragile like this, finally settled against me with her forehead resting in the hollow of my throat. Surprisingly, she doesn't protest.

When we get to the main bedroom, I turn toward the ensuite. I set her down gently on the lid of the closed toilet as I start the water in the large clawfoot tub.

The room fills with steam, blurring the edges of the mirrors. She just watches me with dazed, quiet eyes, looking like she's lost her place in the world now that she's stopped resisting the pull between us. For the first time, she isn't looking for an exit; she's just looking at me.

Once the tub is full, I reach out and lift her again. Her head falls naturally against my shoulder as I lower her into the heat of the water. Any leftover tension finally drains out of her in a single, heavy slump, her muscles going slack as the warmth envelops her.

I linger for a second, my hand resting on the porcelain rim, watching her sink into the water. For a moment, I just let myself look at her without the weight of our history pulling at us. I reach out, brushing a strand of hair behind her ear, before pulling back.

"I'll have some clothes waiting for you on the bed when you're finished," I murmur as I turn to leave the room. "Take your time. I'm not going anywhere."

Chapter 23
ARDEN

A cool breeze and streaks of sunlight streaming in through the open villa window tug me from sleep. My hand reaches across the bed, but all I feel are cold sheets.

Locke must be awake already, as usual. It's really a wonder I woke up before him the night we met... I haven't since. I rub my eyes, dragging my hands down my face as last night rushes back to me.

As much as I try to recall the details, it's mostly a blur. It comes back only in disjointed flashes. His hands pinning mine to marble, the cold countertop against my spine, the scent of whiskey on his breath as he told me he wasn't stopping until I begged. And I did.

I groan softly. *Fuck*. How are we ever going to finish this job now? He could barely handle the sight of me flirting with Luke at the gala, and that was just a harmless conversation. This, though, this just strengthened the pull between us. We've broken down the only wall that kept us focused. How do I go back to being his 'employee' when I know exactly what he looks like when he loses control?

I wonder if he left because he's having the same thoughts. I stare at the ceiling, waiting for the familiar, cold focus of the mission ahead to return, but it's muted by the phantom weight of his hands still pressing against my skin.

As if he read my mind, the door creaks open and Locke strolls into the bedroom in nothing but his boxers, sunlight highlighting the thick black lines covering his chest, torso, and arms. It's easy to forget how much of his body is covered in ink when he's always wearing suits that cover it. It should be illegal to look that good.

He's carrying a massive platter stacked with pastries, a large bowl of fruit, and two tiny coffee cups.

"Espresso!" I squeal.

"I figured you'd want options." His voice is rough with sleep, but his eyes are softer than I've ever seen them. There's a certain sense of contentment about him now that wasn't there before.

He places the tray gently on the bed and climbs in beside me. We both go for the espresso first, using our pointer fingers and thumbs to lift the tiny cups to our lips.

"You know, we're really making a mess of the employee handbook." I gesture between us and the tray. "I keep trying to find a way that we can go back to normal, but I think we've already gone too far for that. There's not a shred of professional distance left to hide behind, is there?"

He shakes his head slowly. "I'm afraid not. But do you really want *normal* when we can be something so much more?"

I hold his gaze, the warmth of the espresso and the sheer nakedness of the man beside me making it hard to even entertain the thought of leaving this bed. I sigh, knowing he's right once again. "Give me the mess over 'normal' any day," I admit, my smile growing wide. "I think I prefer this version of Lochlan Bishop. We both know my life is far from normal as it is."

He smiles too, but that unreadable look returns as he sets his cup down. "The problem with this version," he says, his voice losing its playful edge, "is that he's dreading the part where we have to stop being *this* and go back to being whatever the hell we are out there." He gestures toward the window.

He leans in, his hand resting on the mattress next to my hip. "I don't want to find our way back to normal, because 'normal' was us pretending we didn't want to do this every day. I'm done with the act."

He searches my face, probably waiting to see if I'll agree or try to brush it off, like I have so many times before.

"I want to know that when the threats are over and the job is done, I don't have to ask for permission to be near you anymore. Is that something you can live with?"

I feel the energy in the room shift. The realization settles between us. This has gone from a temporary mess to something that actually has a future. "I think I can manage that," I whisper.

He doesn't pull away. Instead, his gaze intensifies, that unreadable look finally sharpening into something close to regret. "And I know I said you could do jobs like this and make real money, when we met," he says, rubbing the back of his neck, "but I've realized I just can't stand watching you do it."

His hand moves from the mattress to the small of my back, pulling me just an inch closer. "I don't want you to have to play these games just to get by. Let me take care of you, Arden. Let me be the one who makes sure you're set, so you never have to choose between a paycheck and your peace."

I'm quiet for a moment, the weight of his offer, and the possessiveness behind it, settling over me. It's a complete departure from the man who threatened me with jail time to get me to agree to this job in the first place.

"You're serious?" I breathe.

"Dead serious," he murmurs, his thumb tracing the line of my jaw before he finally looks at the clock. Suddenly, the reality of the morning crashes back in. "Shit, but for right now, we still have things to do. Drink your coffee while you get ready."

My brow furrows. "Wait, what? Where are we going?"

He shakes his head, releasing a sigh. "Oh, shit, I ruined the surprise." He reluctantly adds, "Jaxon Wilde is playing at the most historic music venue in Verona tonight. Sound check is in an hour."

He spends the next few minutes explaining how we'll catch up with Jax before the show to get more information about Luke's video and how he got into this little predicament. My jaw hangs open the entire time he talks. Sharp breaths of air catch in my throat with every additional detail he shares.

I move to scoot toward the edge of the bed, ready to get dressed, but before I can get there, Locke grabs my wrist. He mutters, "Just think about what I said, though."

I nod silently as I head into the next room.

When I leave the bathroom 45 minutes later, my jaw instantly hits the floor. "I didn't even know you owned a t-shirt!"

He shoots me an unamused glare from his spot on the edge of the bed. He's handsome in a suit, but in everyday wear? It's giving a slightly older James Dean.

He's in a pair of straight-legged Tom Ford jeans and a white t-shirt with sleeves that hug his biceps just enough to show off his muscular build and the bold Celtic designs woven together around his arms. The whole look is screaming, "Climb on top of me." And the way he's eyeing me tells me he's thinking the same about my outfit choice.

I chose an old band t-shirt that I cut across the top to hang off my right shoulder and tied at the bottom to show just a hint of skin. A tight, black faux leather skirt hugs my curves with wide fishnet tights underneath. Then, I threw on my usual black chunky-heeled boots. I grabbed a flannel shirt from my bag and tied it around my waist as a finishing touch.

"Fuck," he mutters under his breath.

"What's wrong with it?" I ask, brows raised, genuinely confused by his reaction.

"Absolutely nothing," he says, his eyes wandering down the length of my body and back up again. "I'm just not sure I'll be able to focus on anything with you looking like that. Are you trying to torture me?"

"Consider it payback for last night," I say, laughing to myself.

He gives me a devious smile. The look of a man who knows exactly how little I'm protesting what happened between us.

He moves toward me, one hand finding my waist as the other wraps gently around my throat, squeezing just enough to make me forget how to breathe on my own. It's a subtle reminder of his declaration earlier — that he's done with the distance.

Then he kisses me, a slow, intentional press of his lips against mine. "Let's get out of here," he murmurs against my mouth, his voice regaining that professional tone even as his eyes stay soft, "before I decide we have more important things to do, like getting back in that bed."

I nod, my heart pounding against my ribs, and follow him out.

Chapter 24
LOCKE

The matte black Aston Martin purrs beneath my hands as we cut through Verona's narrow streets, drawing just enough attention. After all, it's a bit of a vacation, and I'm sick of giving nosy drivers the chance to eavesdrop. I'm not exactly excited for the day ahead, but I'm eager to be one step closer to putting this job behind us.

Arden shifts beside me, one leg tucked under her, sunglasses perched on her nose like she's about to headline the show herself. She hasn't said a word since we left the villa. Just keeps tapping her fingers against her thigh in time with the music on the radio. Is she nervous?

Every time she speaks of Jaxon, it's with a kind of quiet awe. Remembering that reverence now, her silence makes sense. I'm betting 'nervous' doesn't even come close to describing what she's feeling.

We pull up behind the venue, which is a historic Roman amphitheater that's sometimes still used for concerts, like the one tonight. The ancient stone walls tower high above us, with rows of arches stacked on top of each other and jagged edges near the top where time has worn the stone away.

I might think the sight is stunning if I weren't so focused on why we're here. Not to mention having to watch her ass bouncing in that skirt that's barely covering it, wondering how many rabid crew members I'll have to keep in check today.

"Let's get this over with," I grit out, that thought increasing the annoyance I'm already feeling, as Arden excitedly prances beside me.

"Oh, come on, it's a Jaxon Wilde concert! You can't tell me you're not even a little excited."

"I thought we had already established that I'm not a fan," I reply, making sure she hears the bite of irritation in my voice. "He's just a dumb kid who got too popular too fast and can't handle his shit. We're here for a job; don't forget that."

Arden's shoulders instantly droop, and her gaze drops to the ground. She nods quietly beside me as we continue walking. Right. Jaxon Wilde isn't just some washed-up bad boy to her. He's something more. A symbol, maybe? A lifeline? And I just keep shitting all over it.

"Fuck," I exhale. "I'm sorry. I'm not great at separating work from real life. I know this is all new and exciting for you, but I've been doing this for a long time. Probably too long. I've seen things I can't even say out loud. Done things I wish I could take back. I don't get excited anymore. Everything just makes me... tense. I don't know."

Arden's eyes linger on me, like they're searching for something. There's no judgment there, but for a second, it feels like she's looking beyond the version of me I let everyone else see to the one she saw at the villa... or at least trying.

She gently nods, "Well, I don't know what you've been through, but it sounds like you need a break. Stop being so jaded and live a little!" The way she looks up at me and bites her lip threatens to send me over the edge, adding a quieter, "for me?"

"Keep looking at me like that," I murmur, "and that's not all I'll be doing for you." She giggles lightly, like a schoolgirl seeing her crush in the hallway, and I wish like hell I'd recorded it.

We're let in through a side door leading into a massive dark stone hallway and greeted by the bass thrumming through the concrete floor. A broad-shouldered security guard scrolls through a tablet, asks our names, and slaps neon orange wristbands onto our wrists. Crew members rush past wearing headsets with coiled wires slung over their shoulders. The closer we get, the louder the sound check becomes.

Arden's eyes just get wider and wider. I can practically feel her holding her breath.

Then we turn a corner and step out into the massive arena. The stone walls with built-in seating rise above and around us. The place is completely empty yet somehow alive. Screens flicker, spotlights flash, and a dozen crew members dart across the stage, talking into radios and adjusting cables.

Jaxon Wilde is in the middle of the chaos, barefoot on the concrete stage and skin slick with sweat under the afternoon sun. With the weight of the guitar digging into his shoulder and a mic gripped in one hand, his black button-down hung open to expose the ink across his chest, he's the eye of the storm, and he's loving every second.

Arden comes to a stop beside me, her expression unreadable. She's taking him in, but her lips aren't parted in awe like I thought they'd be. Instead, they're tilted in a faint, amused line. I see the way she tracks his movements, and a sharp spike of jealousy hits me, but I can't deny I love seeing the spark in her eyes.

"Bloody hell," a voice echoes from the stage. Jaxon is staring right at us. He's leaning on the edge of a speaker, mic in one hand, and his eyes zeroed in on Arden. "I didn't think you lot would be here so early."

The British lilt makes his voice sound gritty and rough around the edges. It matches his whole messy, cocky, punk-rocker vibe perfectly. Arden instantly smirks. "We figured you could use an audience."

Jax laughs, hopping off the stage and stalking towards us. "She's a firecracker, this one." He glances at me for half a second before returning his gaze to her. "I might have to keep you 'round, love." He winks at her, and Arden just exhales a short, amused breath, tucking a stray hair behind her ear. It's a human moment, a tiny flicker of nerves, but she doesn't lose her footing.

She stays planted right where she is, looking at him with a cool, expectant expression. He's used to girls melting into a puddle at his feet, but she just holds his gaze.

"Nice to see you again, Jax," I finally interject, fighting to keep my voice even and unbothered. He glances at me, then back at her, dismissing me entirely with a jab of his thumb as he mutters, "Shame you couldn't come alone, love." They share a brief chuckle, but I feel the tension swirling thick in the air now. He didn't faze her with a wink, so now he's trying to get a reaction from me. I thought I'd have to fight off roadies, but I wasn't prepared to stop Jaxon himself. Can I really handle a full day of this?

I step towards him, leaning in close. "She's mine," I whisper so low it almost comes out as a growl, "so cut the shit." For the first time since we got here, he stops smiling. Just stares at me for a second, assessing my reaction. Then, raising his hands in mock surrender, he slowly backs away. "Just havin' a bit o' fun, mate." Before he turns his back on us, I glimpse smug satisfaction on his face. He wanted a reaction, and he got it.

We spend the next several hours listening to Jax warm up and run through his set list. We kill some time talking to his crew, Arden listening intently to the music and singing along. Clapping after each song.

I think I caught her sneaking a picture on her phone and sending it to Lexi. We still haven't learned anything noteworthy about Luke when Jax breaks for food and rest before the show. Arden and I tail him back to the green room, hoping this is our chance.

On the walk over, we agree she can take the lead in the conversation. She's already got his attention, and she seems to find his shameless flirting more entertaining than intimidating.

"Well, what girl wouldn't enjoy a rock star putting on a show for them?" she asks, her voice light and matter-of-fact as we navigate the maze of dark hallways.

I don't answer. She's right, of course. Most girls would live for this kind of attention. But as I watch her easy, confident stride, I realize she isn't just soaking up the compliments. She's matching his energy, and I realize with a sickening jolt that I was right when we got here. Jaxon Wilde isn't just some washed-up bad boy to her. He's still that symbol, that lifeline, and my irritation isn't doing a damn thing to stop it.

When we catch up, he's kicked back on a low leather couch in the green room with his boots up on a coffee table. His shirt is fully unbuttoned now, and his grin is still insufferable. "I was wondering when you'd get here. I saved a spot for ya." He gently pats the open space on the couch next to him.

That gritty English charm makes everything he says sound like a pickup line. Arden plays it cool, matching his arrogant smile with one of her own. She's keeping it light, but I can see the glint in her eye she's trying to hide. The one that says she's exactly where she wants to be. As for me? I'm seconds away from flipping the damn coffee table.

"Drop the act," I finally say, jaw tight. "Let's get to the point here." I guess that got his attention because he instantly shifts in his seat, bringing his boots to the ground as he turns to face Arden.

Her smile fades as she shifts forward, resting her elbows on her knees to lean closer to him, playing good cop to my visibly annoyed one. "Jaxon," she starts, her voice soft but serious, "we really came to talk about Luke. What exactly happened between you two?"

His smile falters, too, and for the first time, I see the sag in his shoulders. The adrenaline that was holding him up seems to drain out of him all at once, leaving his posture slumped and his movements heavy. There are dark shadows etched under his eyes that no amount of stage lighting could hide. He looks utterly exhausted.

"Luke's been on one ever since I called him out in Monaco a few months ago." He glances between us. "He was absolutely smashed at the pub, acting like a total dickhead. Started getting a little handsy with a girl who looked way too young to be there. Definitely too young to handle a guy like Luke when he's like that. Of course, she thought he was amazing, but she was in over her head."

Arden nods in silent understanding, "So you stepped in?"

"Of course I did, I couldn't let him potentially hurt an innocent girl. I had to. I told him to fuck off, loud enough for half the place to turn and look."

He nervously grips the back of his neck. "The next day, I didn't remember a thing that happened after the club. Totally blacked out. The thing is, I know my limit." He glances between the two of us again. "I've spent a lot of time learning how far I can go before I tip over the edge, and I'd only had a few. I didn't slip, Arden, I was pushed. And Luke's fingerprints are all over it."

Arden doesn't look surprised. Her expression is focused and cold.

Her eyes narrow to slits, burning with a fire hotter and stronger than I've ever seen. She doesn't just look angry; she looks like she just accepted a mission with a personal vendetta attached.

"He blocked me on everything, totally ghosted, and the press started sniffing around more. Weird rumors were suddenly springing up." Arden nods again. "And now this footage."

Jax's expression stays hollow. "I don't even remember that night, let alone a camera. Luke's notorious for filming everything under the guise of 'memories,' but I'm starting to wonder how many lives he's actually used those memories to destroy."

"Where can we find him when he's not working?" Arden looks determined, and I have a feeling Luke is going to regret all of this very soon.

Jaxon sighs, "I'm not certain, but he spends a lot of time at this high-roller club in Vegas. That's his favorite playground. You could try it."

Arden huffs out a laugh, shaking her head in disbelief. "Are you kidding me? I didn't even need to leave?" She glares in my direction. "Well, I guess it's time for me to head home."

Jax chimes in, "After the show, right, lovely?" That English charm back in full effect.

"Wouldn't miss it." She winks at him. The display makes me nauseous. It's a performance I'm tired of watching.

"We'll see you out there," I cut in, standing to signal our departure. Jaxon and Arden exchange a glance that hangs in the air far longer than necessary before she and I leave him alone to prepare for the show.

Chapter 25
ARDEN

The bass hits so hard I can feel it in my ribs. Sweat slicks the back of my neck. The lights blur my vision, the crowd roars, and every cell in my body feels like it's vibrating in time with the music.

Jaxon is magnetic on and off the stage. Wild, untouchable chaos wrapped in golden light as he sings songs about angst and rebellion and survival. His eyes scan the crowd, taking time to lock with the gazes of girls who look like they might pass out at any moment. They scream and jump at the chance to share his air; some of them are even crying. It's fascinating, observing it all from our viewpoint next to the stage.

Months ago, I was like all the other girls at this concert. Sitting on my couch, watching videos of Jaxon Wilde performing this exact song and daydreaming about what it might be like to lock eyes with him or hear him say my name. Now I'm backstage at a fucking Roman amphitheater watching him bounce around in front of thousands of people. And this is just a typical day.

Meanwhile, Locke is still staring at me with that "don't test me" look. I know exactly what it's about. He's still annoyed I didn't shut down the rock star's flirting. Even as I try to lose myself in the music, I can't shake the weight of his glare.

"You're still on that?" I ask, unable to hide the hint of a smile playing at my lips. "It was five minutes of harmless banter, Locke. It's not like I was planning a getaway."

He doesn't say anything, but his jaw ticks. It just felt nice to be admired by someone I've respected for a long time. Though my "reminders" don't seem to do anything for his ego.

Jax is definitely playing to the side of the stage where we're standing. Every time his eyes land on me, there's an intentional, heavy focus that says he knows exactly what he's doing. It's hard not to be a little amused by the sheer confidence of it. I half-expect him to address me directly as he lifts the mic again, but he averts his gaze to scan the crowd. "You," he says, pointing. "Third row, red crop top. Yeah, you. Come on up here, love."

The girl is beaming, looking completely shell-shocked by her luck, and Jaxon leans into it with practiced charm. He gives her his full attention, smiling from ear to ear as he asks her to choose his next song. She frantically yells out a single from his first album. It's funny: an hour ago, he was just a guy we were sitting on a couch with, and now he's back to being the public property of a few thousand people.

It's a bit of a reality check. For a second there, I'd let the eye contact go to my head, thinking I was somehow part of the show. Watching him pull a random girl up reminds me that this is just what he does. It's his job to make everyone feel chosen. I glance at Locke, making sure my face is a mask of bored indifference. The last thing I need is his sensing that I was even remotely caught up in the hype.

Locke watches the girl reach the stage, then looks back at me, the 'don't test me' glare finally fading. He leans in close to whisper in my ear. "He's good at that. Making everyone feel like they're the only person in the room. It's quite the show." He brushes a strand of hair behind my ear, his touch lingering. "I think I prefer you back here in the dark with me, though."

Goosebumps rise on my arms like he just slid his fingertips down my spine. He barely even touched me, but my body is acting like it's been waiting all night for this moment.

On stage, Jaxon's energy shifts. The way he pulls the girl in close to dance feels less like a rehearsed stunt and more like they're sharing an actual moment. It's a different vibe... softer, somehow, than performances of his I've seen before. I study them, my head cocked to the side, wondering what the hell I'm actually watching.

When the song ends, he hands her his guitar pick and whispers something in her ear that makes her face light up. Instead of heading back to the floor, she comes beaming over to our side of the stage, clutching the pick like a trophy. She looks completely breathless, wide-eyed and eager for whatever comes next. I can't help but offer her a genuine smile as I introduce myself and Locke; her excitement is too infectious to ignore.

The final chord rings out, vibrating through the stone floor until the lights plunge us into sudden, ringing darkness. The roar of the crowd is deafening, with cheers echoing off the ancient stone walls. It feels like the whole damn city is shaking.

In the dim blue glow of the stage rear, I see Jaxon casually drape an arm around the girl's shoulders, leading her toward the exit with that effortless, rock star swagger.

I'm still wondering who that girl is to him as Locke steps in close behind me. I try to pretend I don't notice and follow the rest of the crew down the hallway, but Locke's hand grabs my wrist, and I know we won't be going anywhere.

I turn to look at him, but he's already backing me into the shadows. Past speakers and black trunks with silver metal edges, until my spine hits something hard and cold.

Locke presses his entire body against mine, pinning me to the wall. The sudden movement steals my breath. "How do I always end up in this position with you?" I gasp as he lifts a hand, his fingers gently dragging along my jawline and down my neck.

He leans in close, a low growl lacing his words as his lips hover near my ear. "Jaxon's a great performer. He can make anyone feel special." His tone is rougher now, lacking the annoyance and leaning into pure possession. "But I think I'm better at reminding you what's real."

I arch my back slightly, letting him feel how much I crave his weight against me. He grinds his hips into me harder, and my fingers curl into his t-shirt.

In an instant, Locke's hands are roaming my entire body. A public display that's far too familiar. He pushes my skirt up enough to slide a hand up my thigh. His fingers slip through the large openings in my tights. Hooking my thong to the side, his palm cups me and finds the slick evidence of how much I've been wanting this.

"Quite the show today," he murmurs, his thumb making a slow, deliberate circle over my clit. I can't help the moan that breaks against his lips.

"All that *harmless* banter," he breathes, his fingers sliding against me, teasing my entrance before moving to circle my clit again. "All those winks and smiles you shot his way."

He doesn't kiss me, though his lips stay inches from mine, sharing my air. His voice isn't cold, but it's thick with a dark, undeniable certainty. "Even after last night, you still think you can play these games? Still want to pretend you don't belong to anyone?"

His fingers stroke faster, a rhythmic, demanding pressure that makes my knees weak. "Well, once again, your dripping pussy says otherwise."

He opens his mouth and bites into the base of my neck, hard enough to make me gasp, the sting immediately blooming into heat. "You're mine," he growls against my skin, the words a simple fact on his tongue.

His hand moves to slip underneath my shirt, his fingers finding my nipple and pinching hard enough to make me whimper.

"Say it," he demands.

"I'm yours." It comes out in a whisper, my voice shaky and full of need. His mouth crashes into mine, a mess of teeth and tongues.

He pulls away just enough to spin me around, his hand firm between my shoulder blades as he guides me down over one of the large black equipment trunks. The cold metal is a shock against my skin.

"I think you need a reminder of that fact," he murmurs, his weight pressing into my back as he crowds me against the case.

I barely have time to grip the edges of the metal trunk before he lifts my skirt completely, baring me to the cool air of the night. Then the first slap lands. A stinging heat that radiates through me.

My breath hitches, a jagged sound that's half-shock and half-surrender. My mind tries to tell me this is too much, even for him, but my body is already arching, instinctively seeking the next strike. The sudden contrast between the cold air around us and the burning on my skin creates a rush that leaves me lightheaded.

He leans down, his chest pressing into my back, his voice a low, heavy vibration against my ear.

"Say it," he demands, his palm rubbing slow circles over the burning skin, waiting. "Who do you belong to?"

"I'm yours, Locke. I... I already said it," I gasp, my head spinning.

Another strike lands. "Again."

"I'm —" The next strike cut me off, stealing the air from my lungs. "Yours."

Another slap landed, punctuated by his low voice. "Again."

"I'm," I gasped, arching into the heat, "yours."

I'm lost in the blur of it all, unable to tell where the pain ends and my need begins. I'm vibrating with a need I can't explain, leaning into the very hands that are causing me pain. It doesn't make sense, but in this dark corner of the stage, the hurt feels like he's pulling me closer to him the only way he knows how. I'm falling apart in his hands, and yet, I've never felt more secure.

The sudden flicker of the lights above us is like a bucket of ice water, dragging me back to reality as Locke's touch turns tender, his large hands smoothing my skirt back into place over my stinging skin.

I straighten my posture and move to walk out with Locke, but he stops me. Without saying a word, one arm wraps around my back, the other slips beneath my knees, lifting me before I can protest.

He carries me to the car, despite my repeated attempts to convince him I can walk. He just silently opens the door and places me in the passenger seat of the flashy sports car he drove us in.

Locke climbs into the driver's seat and starts the engine, the low hum of the car vibrating through me. I watch his profile in the dark, and for the first time, I don't fight the feelings that well up. I'm falling for him.

He flew me to Italy just for a concert. He can say it's 'part of the job' all he wants, but he knew I admired Jaxon from day one. So he put me backstage where I could feel the bass in my ribs. He put me in a room with the man I've looked up to for years. He's spent the past few days proving he knows exactly what I love... and making sure I know he's the one who can give it to me.

Seeing the quiet intensity in his eyes now, I'm finally understanding that his possessive nature is his way of holding on to what's important to him.

Chapter 26
LOCKE

The drive back to the villa is pure torture. I'm starting to think a driver would've been the smarter move after all. I'd much rather cozy up with her in the backseat of an SUV than be here white-knuckling the steering wheel.

Arden winces slightly as she adjusts in her seat. Thoughts of the way she looked bent over that black trunk flood my mind. Fingers gripping around the edges as I made her say it over and over again, "I'm yours." The words echo in my mind, too.

The mounting pressure in my jeans is making it impossible to think, let alone drive. I don't know why she has this much power over me, but it's becoming a huge problem.

Now my only goal is getting us back to the villa in one piece so I can show her exactly what it means to belong to me. Backstage was a reminder. Not exactly a punishment, just me reclaiming what was always mine to begin with. A precursor to the way I'm going to ruin her tonight. Foreplay, if you will.

All I know is as soon as this car stops, I plan to lock the world out and leave my mark on every single place Jaxon's eyes dared to look today.

She doesn't wait for me. Before the engine even cuts off, she's a blur of motion heading for the front door. She's not fast enough to get past me, though. I'm already there, blocking her path, my pulse thrumming with a lack of control that feels almost dangerous.

"You really think I'm going to let you off that easy?"

She snaps her head in my direction. "What, that wasn't enough for you? You're not going to tell me to go to bed?"

A low, dry laugh scratches at my throat. "Not this time. Not even close."

My gaze meets her ocean-blue eyes, and I catch a flicker of flame there. I drink in that look. I don't think I could ever get enough.

She moves closer, crowding me until the backs of my thighs meet the hood of the car. I sit against it, the still-running engine warming the surrounding space. The height of her boots brings her close enough to hook her arms around my neck and pull me into a kiss.

Her tongue slides against mine with a desperate, tangling heat that tells me she wants this just as much as I do. I lock my hands around her waist, pulling her flush against me and grinding my hips into hers so there's no mistaking exactly what she's doing to me. No mistaking how much I need her. Right here, right now.

I shift my grip to her shoulders, the pressure firm as I guide her down until she's kneeling on the gravel in front of me. She stays there, blue eyes wide and almost innocent as they gaze up at me. It's fucking magic.

The car's headlights illuminate her face as I grab a fistful of her hair and tug, tilting her head back. Her mouth falls open, eyes still locked on mine. The sight of her waiting is enough to send me over the edge.

I inch closer, tugging my zipper down to finally free myself from the suffocating grasp of my jeans. I let out a low, rough exhale as the pressure finally lets up, replaced by a much better kind of tension. "Look at you, giving me exactly what I need. Good girl."

I can see a hint of heat creeping into her cheeks, and a small smile forming, as I place the head of my cock in her mouth, still ready and waiting.

She doesn't miss a beat, instantly swirling her tongue over the tip, collecting the taste of me in her mouth, and wrapping a hand around the base of my cock. At first, she's teasing; sliding her tongue and hand along the length of my shaft at an infuriatingly calm pace.

My breath hitches when she finally seals her lips around me and takes in my full length. "Fuck, Arden," I breathe, "you look even more beautiful with my cock in your mouth."

I curl my fingers in her hair, gripping tight to keep her mouth exactly where I want it, controlling her every move. She lets out a moan around me, triggering a low groan that escapes my lips before I can stop it. I'm suddenly driven by a relentless need to lose control, even as I fight to keep her completely under mine.

I pull her head toward my body, forcing my cock deeper into her mouth until I feel it hit the back of her throat. Reality feels out of focus as I settle into a rhythm. Thrusting hard and fast until the world narrows to nothing but breath and motion.

Tears stream down her face, mascara staining her cheeks in thick black smudges. Then she gags, and I unravel entirely. I can't even warn her before the thick streams of cum shoot into the back of her throat, filling her mouth before she swallows it all.

The tension in my muscles disappears, and I can finally ease the tension in my hand, releasing my grip on her hair. I'm still drifting back to earth when she rocks back on her heels, looking up at me with a smile on her face that's nothing short of lethal.

"I'm yours," she says, her words coated with wicked amusement, "or do I need to tattoo your name on me like a luggage tag for you to finally believe it?"

"Careful," I rasp. "I might just take you up on that. I've got a very specific spot in mind for the ink."

I watch that wicked smile of hers falter for a split second as I reach for her. Before she knows what's happening, I'm already sweeping her into my arms. My hands wrap around the backs of her thighs as I carry her through the villa doors. The scene feels almost like déjà vu, but this time I head straight for the bedroom.

I set her lightly on the edge of the mattress, not bothering to pull back the quilted comforter as I guide her down onto her back. Her shirt slides off and is thrown to the floor in one fluid motion. Then, I'm tugging her skirt to her ankles too, and soon she's in nothing but fishnets. They look better on her than any tattoo ever could; I'm more than happy to work around them.

Taking in the sight of her, almost naked in the moonlight, my mouth nearly waters. Her exposed nipples peak in the cool night air, and I can't resist leaning down to take one between my teeth. The quick taste is just enough to evoke a sound that lands somewhere between a gasp and a moan.

I raise her legs into the air, spreading her wide open in front of me, and reach between her thighs. She's still slick with need for me, just like she was at the concert.

I slowly slide two fingers inside of her, gently massaging her inner walls as I admire the way her wavy hair falls around her face. She moans my name, gripping the sheets, and I take my fingers back.

Making sure she's watching, I slide them into my mouth and lick myself clean. Her sweet taste alone is stirring that primal hunger in my chest again. "I wasn't lying when I said you're delicious; it almost seems criminal not to have a taste."

I want to play, to tease, but the primal — no, feral — side of me can't wait any longer. It aches to feel the tight grip of her pussy squeezing my cock.

She doesn't respond right away, just gazes up at me, gently biting her lip, waiting for whatever comes next as she watches me kick off my jeans. As I move back toward her, she reaches out, her fingertips grazing my hip.

"You're doing a lot of talking for someone who's supposed to be claiming me," she challenges.

A dry chuckle vibrates in my chest as I lean in, shadowing her completely. "Patience, darling. I was just appreciating the view first."

I can feel her shaking with anticipation as I roll her onto her stomach, sliding her legs out with my knees to position her on all fours in front of me. I let out a deep moan at the sight of her perfect ass and cunt on full display. I grip her hips, then drag my hands down over the light imprint of my hand still lingering from earlier.

"Keep being a good girl for me, Arden. You might get a treat."

She lets out a small, needy hum of approval. Unable to wait any longer, I place the head of my cock at her entrance. Then, slowly, inch my way in. The squeeze is so perfect I can barely contain myself. Everything about her makes me want to lose control.

I take my time, letting my hands roam from her hips to her ass, spreading her wide as I thrust in and out at a steady pace. I lean forward, my mouth hovering just above her as I let a slick thread of saliva bridge the gap between us. I use my thumb to spread it over her hole before pressing it inside.

Her moan reverberates through me, threatening to tear me apart, and I watch as she grabs fistfuls of the sheets. I reach my other hand around to trace circles over her clit, and her inner walls squeeze my cock. It's clear how close she is, too.

I continue my rough thrusts in and out of her as she arches her back, begging for more.

"Fuck, Locke. I'm so —" She whimpers between moans. She doesn't have to finish her sentence for me to know exactly what she means.

"Cum for me, Arden. I need to feel that tight pussy squeeze around me again."

Her answering moan echoes through the villa. Her body goes wild, hips bucking against my thrusts, until we both topple over the edge together.

As the frenzy fades, leaving only the sound of our ragged breathing and the two of us lying in the dark together, I reach for the familiar crutch of calculated distance I use to keep the world out. But my fingers come up empty.

I've spent my entire life obsessed with being the one who always has control; the man who writes the narrative. But between her moans and the primal need that hooked its claws in me, I seem to have truly lost it. She hasn't just unraveled me; she's made me unrecognizable, even to myself.

Except, for once, that thought isn't accompanied by fear. Just a strange sense of clarity. There's something here with her that feels entirely worth the risk of getting close and, for the first time, actually expecting someone to stay.

Chapter 27
ARDEN

Fresh espresso is the first thing I see when I open my eyes. Sitting on the nightstand, still steaming hot. Underneath the tiny mug is a piece of paper with something scrawled on it in black ink. I pick up the drink with one hand and the note with the other, taking a sip while I read: *I promised you a treat. Get ready and meet me at the door.*

I jump out of bed, downing the shot. Getting dressed is easy, I already had a black t-shirt and my favorite ripped jeans set aside for today. I swap my usual boots for high-top Converse, throwing on a black beanie and a swipe of mascara to finish the look. I'm ready to go in ten minutes flat. That has to be a record.

As I reach the bedroom door, I realize I'm forgetting something. I double back, rushing to my duffel bag to retrieve the tarnished gold chain from the inside pocket. I shove it in my jeans as I exit into the hallway.

Locke is seated in a chair near the front door, a cigar balanced between his fingers. He's in a t-shirt for the second day in a row, the cotton stretched taut across his chest and shoulders in a way that a suit could never touch. My pulse quickens, and I have to consciously force my gaze upward from the defined curve of his bicep to his face.

It's a rare sight, Locke unbuttoned and unguarded. But I know the clock is ticking. The job will be waiting for us back in Vegas, and I have a feeling it'll turn him back into the 'all business' man I first met. I'm going to enjoy every moment of the more relaxed version of him while I can.

As soon as he notices me, he stands. "I didn't know you owned sneakers."

"Well, I didn't know you owned more than one t-shirt," I quip back.

The usual edge in his expression has melted into something softer, and his lips part in a faint, amused line. "I promised you a treat. Jax is already on his way to his next show, and Nate's taking care of everything back home, so I thought we'd just enjoy one more day in Verona together."

I nod, a smile turning up the corner of my lips, and follow him out. There's no driver and no car waiting. I shoot him a puzzled look. "No car?"

"I thought we could walk today," he says with a shrug. He offers his arm, a silent command for me to intertwine mine. I accept the invitation as we continue into the nearby square.

We spend the morning and early afternoon wandering through piazzas and exploring local markets. Snaking through crowds, stopping to admire the flowers, produce, and souvenirs, and occasionally pausing for a glass of wine. There's something about the cobblestone streets and views of the river winding through the city that makes the air itself feel romantic. Like we've stepped into a dream.

When Locke approaches me with a bouquet of red roses, orange zinnias, and deep purple chrysanthemums wrapped in brown paper, the breath hitches in my throat.

I try to summon a sharp remark. The kind I've used for years to keep people at arm's length, but the words won't come. My shoulders loosen, and a terrifying warmth seeps through the cracks of my composure. He's seen the calculated side of me. The girl who looked at him and saw a mark instead of a man. Yet he's still here, offering me flowers instead of following through on his jail threat.

He hands me the bouquet and takes my free hand, leading me out of the piazza toward a blacked-out SUV parked nearby. "I have one last surprise that does actually require a vehicle."

I don't argue or ask questions. I just bury my face in the flowers, inhaling their sweetness as I follow him into the backseat. For the first time, we don't even try to keep our distance. His arm settles around me, and I lean into his warmth as we ride through the streets of Verona.

The driver drops us off at the edge of an enormous lake. Its surface is a flawless mirror of turquoise. I've never seen a more breathtaking view. Locke takes my hand and leads me down a narrow path as the sun sinks lower in the sky.

We reach a small, secluded patch of grass where a giant white blanket is sprawled across the ground. String lights are wrapped around the trunk of a nearby tree, casting a soft golden glow over the meal spread before us. A charcuterie board overflowing with fruit, cheeses, and sliced meats. Several bottles of wine and two glasses sit nearby.

My throat goes dry. I want to tell Locke how beautiful this is, how utterly romantic and completely unexpected. I try, but nothing comes out.

Suddenly it all comes rushing back to me. All the birthdays that passed without even a card, the milestones without a moment of celebration, the countless times I ate alone, walked home in the dark, or realized that not one person in the room actually cared if I was there.

All I can do is stare at the scene in front of me, then back at him. Hot tears spill down my cheeks, despite my best effort to hold them back.

Locke's brow furrows as his eyes dart between the picnic and me. "Is everything okay?"

"No one's ever done anything like this for me. No one." I let out a sigh, dabbing my eyes. "I'm not even sure I've ever been on a real date. But this... this isn't just a date. It's amazing."

He looks genuinely shocked by that confession. Maybe I've said too much. But I don't care. I want him to know how much this means to me.

Locke sits in an open space near the food, and I follow, settling beside him. He pours two glasses of wine as I pop a grape into my mouth, watching the sunset paint the water in gold and coral. It's the most magnificent thing I've ever seen, maybe even better than the desert sunsets back home. I'd always thought they were the most beautiful things in the world.

It takes me a few moments to realize that Locke is staring at me. I give him a sideways glance. "...Why are you looking at me like that?"

"Just enjoying the view."

I nearly choke on my wine. "Okay, that was the cheesiest thing I've ever heard."

He just smiles. "What can I say? You've brought out a side of me I haven't seen in a long time. I'm leaning into it."

"A long time," I repeat softly, the words hanging between us. "What happened to him, Locke? The version of you that used to be like this?"

Locke hesitates, his gaze darting toward the horizon. "Oh, just my whole life, really."

Despite the smile playing on my face, a wave of sadness washes over me. "Same."

His eyes match my sadness now, too. "Yeah, growing up with a dad in the mob will do that to you. It's not quite like the movies, but it isn't normal, either."

I blink, eyes wide. "The mob? I didn't peg you as Italian."

"I'm not. The Irish have a mob too, you know."

"Ooh, an Irishman? Too bad you didn't get the accent. That would be hot."

Locke gives me a flat look. "As I was saying," he exhales, "my dad was pretty high up. Our family was respected, wealthy, and protected. Being the oldest, he expected me to take over the family business. He started training me from the time I was sixteen. We ran nightclubs and private event venues — at least, that was the legal side. Luxury hospitality for high-end clients. But that all ended when the FBI finally caught up with him. They hit him with RICO charges. Money laundering, drug trafficking, conspiracy... all the greatest hits. They came for him in the middle of the night. Didn't even bother knocking, just busted right through the door. I remember my mother offering coffee to all the agents while they tore the place apart." He shakes his head, smiling to himself. "He's been in federal prison ever since."

I stay silent for a moment, letting the new information settle before asking, "So what happened? To the business, I mean."

"I took over after he went away. A little sooner than expected, but I did my best. Back then, I just wanted to make him proud, but I was determined to make it fully legitimate. Didn't want me or, worse, Nate ending up where he is. So, I stopped the laundering and the drugs and kept the entertainment for a while."

"I have to say, the idea of you planning parties is hilarious. But how'd you go from that to PR?"

"Excuse me? I throw great parties," he shoots back with a mock glare. "But I only managed events for a while. Mostly for celebrities and other high-end clients. Producers, politicians, the odd millionaire. It was fine until people like Luke started showing up. I thought walking away from the mob was enough, but I was wrong. The industry still attracts the same rot. People who actually make organized crime look tame. I couldn't stomach being so close to it anymore, so I rebranded the business as Bishop Strategies. I swore I was going to actually help people." He lets out a dry laugh. "Now I just help them cover up their lies."

I swirl what's left of the wine in my glass, watching the deep red liquid catch the fading light. "You help them clean up their messes," I murmur more to myself than him, "I usually just make them."

Locke huffs out a quiet laugh, but his eyes stay on me. "You ever get tired of that?"

"Of what? Messes?"

"No. The running."

I glance at him, then back at the water. "That depends on what or who is chasing me."

That smirk is back on his face, and I can't help but admire the way the setting sun frames it with golden rays. "So, what about you? Lexi? What's the story there?"

I refill my glass and take a deep breath. "We've been best friends for... well, forever. She lived in the apartment next door. We've always been there for each other — ride or die. It was us against the world. So, when she needed help with Zoe, we moved in together."

Locke studies me for a long moment. "Can you finally tell me what she does for a living, or is it still classified information?"

A giggle, an actual giggle, escapes me. I had completely forgotten about his questions when we met. "She's a stripper. Exotic dancer. Whatever," I say waving my hand at him. "We only keep it secret from Zoe. Also, before you jump to conclusions, she doesn't work in some sleazy, run-down hole-in-the-wall. She performs at one of the best clubs in Vegas."

He doesn't say anything, just nods like he's waiting for me to go on.

"The money is good, but I worry about her. She's a hopeless romantic, but most men can't handle being with someone in her line of work."

Locke keeps nodding. Gazing thoughtfully down at his glass, "And you? Your family?"

That word makes my heart drop. "Just Lexi. My dad disappeared when I was twelve. He was mixed up with the wrong people... cartel business, I think. I never knew the details. After that, it was just my mom and me for a while. She was an addict my whole life, and it only got worse when he was gone. She overdosed a few months after I turned eighteen."

Locke's eyes shine in the golden light as mine rise to meet them again, gold flickering in the whiskey brown. It feels like he's seeing straight through me.

I'm the first to break the gaze, reaching into the pocket of my jeans. When I pull my hand out, a gold chain with a tarnished cross dangles from it, the sunlight glinting off its edges. I hold it out to him as he raises his eyebrows, clearly surprised. "I think this belongs to you."

Locke nods and takes the cross, running his thumb over it. "Didn't think I'd see this again. It was my dad's... and his dad's before that. So, thank you."

"Yeah, well, I didn't mean to take something sentimental. Not really my thing. Just wanted to make sure you got it back."

Locke tucks the chain into his pocket, eyes lingering on mine.

For a long moment, neither of us speaks. The string lights hum softly above us, and the air smells like wine and salt and something almost sweet. He reaches out, brushing his thumb over my hand. "You could've kept it," he whispers.

I swallow, feeling warmth spread through me. "Why would I do that? It's special to you."

He doesn't respond right away, just leans back on his elbow, still looking at me like I'm part of the view. I look out at the view, too, as the last rays of sun dip below the horizon.

His voice is nearly a whisper a few moments later. "Have you thought about what I said yesterday?"

I nod. "I have."

"And?" Locke sighs.

"This has been my identity throughout my entire adult life. I don't think I'll know what to do with myself." I shift closer to him.

He studies me thoughtfully, considering his answer. "I don't know, but whatever you want to do, you'll have the ability to do it."

He sips a fresh glass of wine. "Start a business, a charity, read books, travel the world. I truly don't give a fuck. Just let me take care of you."

"So, what, we'll move in together? Or are you going to pay my rent too?" I challenge, narrowing my eyes at him.

"Whatever you want, Arden. I mean it. I will support any decision you make."

I look away from him, back toward the lake. The word 'support' sounds like a foreign language. My life has been a series of carefully crafted walls. Keeping people out, keeping myself upright, making sure I never leaned too hard on anything that could give way. To let him do this isn't just about the money or the freedom; it's about handing over the heavy armor I've worn since I was a child. It's terrifying. If I stop being the girl who survives, who am I?

But then I consider the weight of the last few years. The constant looking over my shoulder, the exhaustion of the hustle. I look at Locke, really look at him. He isn't offering a golden cage; he's offering a floor that won't give out from under me. For the first time, I wonder what I could actually *be* if I weren't always just trying to stay afloat.

I nod slowly, the tightness in my chest finally beginning to uncoil. "Okay," I whisper, the word feeling heavier and more honest than anything I've ever said. "I guess I can live with that."

And for the first time in a long time, I stop pretending I don't want to be seen.

Chapter 28

LOCKE

The Vegas sun is brutal, not like the gold-drenched warmth of Verona. This kind of heat makes you feel like you're walking into the depths of hell. I can see heatwaves radiating from the shimmering asphalt on the runway; it looks like it could melt beneath us.

I spent the entire flight replaying the conversation we had yesterday, dissecting every word until I was sure I hadn't imagined it. She's mine now. Not only has she agreed to the title, but she actually agreed to let me in. She agreed to let me provide, to let me be the one she leans on when the world is too loud. I stare out at the vast wasteland of heat and melting asphalt and feel a savage sort of satisfaction. The walls are finally down, and I'm never giving her a reason to build them back up.

Arden slides on her sunglasses, silent beside me as the plane door opens. No more cobblestones and wine; now it's just the desert sun, neon lights, and the man we came here to find.

"You ready?" I ask, watching her stand and smooth her outfit. She doesn't look back; her gaze is fixed on the view of the Vegas skyline outside the open door. "Always."

On the flight, she made me promise that our first stop would be her condo. She can't go another day without seeing Lexi and Zoe. I almost called her dramatic; it hasn't been that long, but another part of me envies it. That kind of love leaves an ache when it's gone, a feeling of being incomplete.

I'm not sure I've ever really understood that kind of longing. Even with Nate, our bond is just... there. It's steady. I've never felt that frantic need to get back to someone just to feel whole again. It makes me wonder if I've been missing out, or if I'm just now realizing how much space one person can take up in your heart.

Lexi is a handful, but she's exactly the kind of person Arden needs in her corner. Mostly, I'd do anything to see her face light up again. At the concert, she looked free. Like nothing had ever touched her. I know better but letting myself believe it for one second made me feel alive. I'd do anything to see her look like that again.

When we pull into her building's parking garage, Arden doesn't wait. She's out of the car before I've even shifted into park. Her heels echo on the concrete as she bolts for the elevator. I stay behind for a minute longer, hands still gripping the wheel.

She didn't invite me up... but she didn't say I couldn't follow, either. I've never been great at fitting into other people's lives, especially when they're as complex as hers. And now, back on her turf, I feel the familiar twinge of unease creeping up my spine.

By the time I reach the door, I hear muffled voices filtering through the walls. High-pitched female laughter accompanied by the unmistakable squealing of a child. It's the sound of a home; a world I'm not entirely sure I belong in, but here I am anyway.

I reach for the handle, but a prickle of unease along the back of my neck stops me. I don't turn around immediately; I stop to glance at the polished brass of the unit number next door, using it as a distorted mirror.

There at the far end of the hallway, leaning against the wall of the stairwell, I can make out the outline of a dark figure. It would be so easy to walk right past them, the black hoodie masking their shape in the shadows. I let my hand drop from the lever and slowly turn around.

His frame looks broad and imposing in the narrow space. But it's the lower half of his face that I recognize. The dark gaiter pulled up over his mouth and nose, featuring the stark, white jaw of a printed skull. It's a piece of gear I've seen him wear on his bike a thousand times, a macabre mask that makes him look less like a man and more like a reaper. Fitting for his current position.

Seb.

He doesn't move. He doesn't wave. He just stands there, his gaze fixed on the door I'm about to enter. I told him to watch Lexi, but seeing him like this — a silent, masked sentinel haunting a residential hallway — reminds me that Seb doesn't do anything halfway. He does excessive. Most of all, he does effective.

I take a breath, the warm memory of the flight cooling instantly. I want to go in and find that peace again, but Seb's eyes are on me now.

He finally moves, a slow wave of two fingers from his temple. He pulls the skull gaiter down around his neck, revealing a smudge of a grin and a sharp glint in his eyes.

"Holy shit, bro," I mutter, keeping my voice low enough that it won't carry through Arden's door. "I told you to watch over her, not stalk her like a literal psycho. You look like you're waiting to harvest someone's soul."

Seb's grin widens, sharp and unrepentant. "I'm just being thorough. You didn't specify the distance." Jerking his chin toward the door he adds, "The firecracker sisters are inside. They're safe and they're loud."

I grin, shaking my head at him. "Go home, Seb. Get some sleep. Or at least take off the mask before a neighbor calls the cops."

He just shrugs, pulling his hood down again, already receding back into the shadows of the stairwell without another word. He's gone before I even turn around.

I push the door open, the sound of Zoe's laughter and the scent of pancakes and coffee hitting me all at once.

"Locke, is that you?" Arden's voice calls out, bright and expectant.

"It's me," I call back, locking the deadbolt. *Wouldn't want any psycho stalkers getting bold.*

I stand there for a second, my back to the door, just breathing in the change of atmosphere. For the first time in weeks, the air feels different. The tension is gone, leaving room to breathe, and enjoy the company around me.

When I round the corner into the kitchen, the sight nearly breaks me. Arden is engulfed in a chaotic three-way hug with Lexi and Zoe, a tangle of limbs and laughter that looks so private I feel like an intruder.

Lexi catches my eye over Arden's shoulder. She looks exactly like the firecracker I met before we left. Her bright orange hair is down around her shoulders today, but those eyes are still sharp and assessing even as she squeezes her friend. She gives me a look that says she's thankful I brought Arden back, but she'll still kill me if I breathe wrong.

Zoe breaks away first, her eyes wide as she looks at me like I'm some sort of giant who's wandered into her playhouse. "Is he staying for breakfast?" she chirps. Before I can respond, she's back to tugging on Arden's hand, demanding to know if we brought back any "Italian treasures."

Watching Arden pouring coffee, ruffling Zoe's hair, falling into a rhythm with Lexi again, I realize this is the weight she agreed to let me carry. It's not just her; it's this entire, beautiful, messy life.

I find a seat at the island, feeling out of place in my tailored suit against the backdrop of half-eaten pancakes and a child's chaos, but for the first time in my life, I don't want to be anywhere else.

When breakfast is over and Zoe is off to school, the mood shifts again. The table that held pancakes and playful banter has now stiffened into something like a briefing station. I sit back as Arden lays it all out: the gala, the horror show of an after-party, everything Jaxon said, and why we're back in Vegas even though our work is nowhere near done.

Lexi listens intently, clenching her coffee cup between white knuckles as her best friend gives her the play-by-play. Only interrupting to ask questions or beg for the juiciest details.

When Arden finishes her story, there's nothing but silence. Then Lexi leans forward, eyes sharpening. "Well then, what's our first move?"

Chapter 29
ARDEN

After explaining to Lexi that I appreciate her willingness to help, but there's no way in hell I would ever take it, she reluctantly agreed to only help me pick the clothes I'll wear for my 'accidental' run in with Luke. It has to *look* accidental, at least. But more importantly, I have to look like I belong in the same high-roller lounge as him. Without Locke.

And I'll need a damned good story if this plan has any hope of working in my favor. But that's Locke's job to figure out. He's been on the phone all day, coordinating the details.

Hours pass as we burn through one outfit after another. I pace the length of Lexi's bedroom, my bare feet almost silent on the polished concrete, trailing discarded silk and hangers in my wake. My reflection keeps changing, but none of the versions of me feel right. They're either too desperate or too forgettable.

Lexi bounces around, her energy infuriatingly contagious, tossing a pair of designer pumps onto the bed while I struggle to toe the line between effortless and unforgettable. Each look ends with the same frustrated sigh and a pile of fabric on the floor. My thoughts flick back and forth between the current moment and the task ahead.

Locke confirmed the name of the lounge Luke frequents with some of his connections around town. In true douchebag fashion, Luke prefers the most exclusive club in the entire city. Tucked away on the second floor of a lavish casino in the middle of the strip, reserved for only the most elite players. It should be easy enough to get his attention, but if he gets suspicious? I'm not sure how that will end for me. My chest tightens at the thought.

The realization hits me as I'm standing in Lexi's closet. She zips me into a blur of red lace and silk. A dress far too scandalous for a normal day. It hangs off my frame with the suggestive appearance of lingerie, making me feel exposed even though I'm technically dressed.

"This is heavy, Lex," I mutter, watching my reflection. "If I mess this up, if he catches on to what we're doing... he has the kind of pull that can make people disappear from the map. Not just Jaxon, but all of us."

Lexi stops adjusting my shoulder strap and meets my eyes in the mirror. She doesn't look panicked or nervous; she just looks focused. "He's a predator with a publicist, Arden. That's all."

She turns me around, gripping my shoulders firmly. "Yeah, he's clearly deep into some dark, twisted shit. That party? I can't believe what you told me. That's exactly why he's going to fall for this. He thinks he's untouchable. He's arrogant enough to think you're just another girl he can put under his spell."

I swallow hard, my pulse thrumming in my temples. "I just need to get it right. Jaxon could lose everything. I can't let myself be the reason that happens."

"You won't," she insists, her voice steadying me. "You're doing this because men like Luke Holloway deserve to be exposed for the pieces of shit they really are. Don't let the fame intimidate you. He's just another mark, Arden. And you've never missed a mark in your life."

She lets go with a final, encouraging pat and turns to hunt for the right earrings. I try to match her confidence, but my mind is still racing. Luke Holloway is an international icon.

I know Locke has my back; he's made that clear. But as I examine my reflection, I feel the heavy weight of that promise. If this goes south, I'm not just risking myself anymore. I don't want to be the reason Locke goes to war.

My spiral ends abruptly when Locke himself walks through the door. He slows his pace, his gaze traveling over the dress with a heavy intensity that makes the air in the room feel thinner. "Did Lexi help you find the right weapon?" he asks, his voice low.

"I think so," I reply, forcing my voice to stay level. I smooth the silk over my hips and meet his eyes. "We've got the look. Now, I just have to make sure he notices it. If I can get him talking at the lounge, do you think he'll take the bait and invite me up to his suite?"

Locke drags a hand through his hair, his eyes lingering on the low dip of the neckline with a look that is equal parts heat and pure frustration. "With you wearing that? There's no doubt in my mind."

"He's in a comped penthouse on the top floor. It's guarded, invite-only. You won't get anywhere near the elevators without his clearing the way. We're banking entirely on the run-in at the lounge."

I give him a silent nod. My eyes shift to gaze out the window. Neon lights bounce across my reflection, the city blurring like a dream.

He steps in close, coming up behind me to wrap his arms around my shoulders. I place my hand on his wrist. "I know a guy, a hacker, one of my dad's old buddies. He's been at this for a long time, and he agreed to help us out. We have all the tech details sorted; all you have to do is gain Luke's trust enough to get close to his electronics. I'll give you all the tools you need tomorrow."

I nod again. "We'll be in your ear the whole time, and we'll be able to hear, too. I pulled some strings and got a room on the same floor. If you need me for any reason, I can be there in minutes."

I turn my back to the window, moving his hands to rest on my hips, and look up into his eyes. "I'm okay, Locke. You don't need to worry about me." I say it with a shrug, unsure if I'm trying to convince him or myself. Either way, I don't think it's working. "I'm just ready to get in there and get this done. We can't let Luke release a video of Jaxon doing God-knows-what while he was blacked out. We can't let his fans think it's something he chose."

Locke strokes a hand down my spine. "We'll get it taken care of. I know you said I don't need to worry about you, but I will anyway."

I look at him, my brow furrowed, ignoring the shiver that travels through me. "I told you, I'm perfectly fine."

Locke's hands tighten on my hips. "I know, it's just once you step in there, there's no going back," he murmurs.

I nod, and a part of me wishes we could stay here forever.

Chapter 30
LOCKE

Back in the familiarity of Vegas, Arden, Lexi, and Zoe slipped right back into their everyday routine. I've watched them from the sidelines for the past few days, struck by the simplicity of their life together. We have a plan to execute and a man to expose, but in the waiting, they've just been the same little family they've always been.

I left the ladies to themselves and stepped into Arden's bedroom for one last brief with Seb over the phone. He's been lying low since we arrived, and I've kept it that way. After his stunt in the stairwell, I wasn't about to invite him into their home. Although, frankly, I've been too buried in prep to notice, or care, if he's still lurking in the shadows.

For the last forty-eight hours, he's helped me track down the hacker and the tools we'll need to take down Luke Holloway. He's been the one running surveillance and mapping the casino's layout. With the tech dialed in and the layouts memorized, the plan feels as solid as it's going to get.

Sleep hadn't really been part of my schedule. Neither had eating. I've been holed up alone, every hour bleeding into the next until the neon buzzing outside the windows felt like the only thing keeping me awake.

Tiernan, one of my dad's old mob connections who's somehow still alive, is my ticket to tapping into the casino's internal security system. The man is a legend. Decked out in a sharp suit and even sharper paranoia, he's a goddamn artist when it comes to breaking into complex security networks. He's agreed to crack the code to the casino's security cameras, so we'll have eyes everywhere.

Hacking the security feed gives us a full visual of every corner of the lounge, and her earpiece will allow us to keep in contact the entire time. I even convinced Tiernan to reroute the casino's backup signal so no one could trace the interference back to us.

So now, here we are, watching her enter this giant neon playground from a hotel room high above the club she's headed to. On the cameras, she looks small. But even through the video feed, there's a sharpness in her posture that makes my heart race.

As she drifts through the casino, light catches on gleaming stones hanging from giant chandeliers and bounces off her jewelry. It's a palace built for people who think they'll never lose. She blends in perfectly.

Word on the street is that Luke will be here all day. Gambling, drinking, parading around like he owns the place. Arden's job is simple, on paper: just catch his eye and wait for the right moment to flatter him. I feel the knots in my stomach forming already. The thought of watching her flirt with another man yet again makes me want to end this entire operation.

I could walk in there myself and settle this with my fists, but that would just be another headline Luke could spin in his favor. We need a clean execution. Watching Arden work her way into his orbit is torture, but it's the only way that guarantees we walk away with his career in our hands. I'm not here for theatrics; I'm here to collapse his whole empire.

I watch her walk casually into the high-roller lounge, turning heads the entire way. The security guard by the door follows her with his eyes as she sits at a blackjack table near the center of the room. So it isn't just me... is everyone this mesmerized by her?

Well, how could they not be? That red silk dress clings to her like it was custom-made, threadlike straps glinting against her skin. A black leather jacket is draped over her shoulders, and she wears her usual lace-up heeled boots. Only, they're not her usual? No, these have silver rivets and spikes trailing down each heel. She looks more lethal than ever. I force myself to look away as the pressure of my cock, hard against my zipper, mounts. *Fuck me.*

Scanning the cameras, I spot Luke sitting at a table in the room's far corner. His head is down, focused on the cards in front of him, but when he looks up, his line of sight will lead directly to her.

"If you can hear me, tuck your hair behind your ear," I say, my voice low and steady. She does. A small burst of satisfaction flares in my chest. *Oh, this could be fun.*

"Okay, now bend down and tie your shoe. Turn a little this way." I see her subtly shake her head on the camera. "Get back to work," she mutters, sliding a neat stack of chips to the center of the blackjack table she's chosen.

It's then that I notice Luke has glanced up from his game. He's staring straight at her. "Oh, I think you've got an admirer." I murmur. "Game on." I can't see her face from this angle, but her body goes still. Through the mic, I hear her suck in a slow breath and release it, steadying herself.

She lifts her cards, hiding behind them just as Luke pushes his seat back. He cashes out, says something to the dealer, and then he's stalking toward her.

Watching them through screens like this, I feel detached. Like I'm not here at all. Like I'm watching a scene straight out of a nature documentary. The lion spots his prey, completely unaware that the creature waiting for him isn't prey at all. She's a predator disguised as something timid and harmless, a wolf in sheep's clothing, and he's running straight into her trap.

Chapter 31
ARDEN

I notice him standing up just after Locke mentions my admirer. I try not to stare. Trying not to draw attention, I catch his eyes narrowing. It's a look I've seen before, a predator stalking its prey, but there's something darker behind it.

Maybe it's just the alcohol. He sways slightly as he walks, trying to play it off as an overconfident swagger. The idea of his being drunk raises the hair on the back of my neck. If there's one thing I've learned over the years, it's that a drunk asshole can be very good or very bad. Now I just have to figure out which one he'll be today.

The casino is a whirlwind around me. Slot machines trill and chime, chips clatter on the table, and laughter bursts like gunfire. The air smells like money, expensive cologne, and a hint of desperation. It's a familiar symphony I've known my whole life. For most, it might distract, but the chaos is just white noise to me. It drowns out everything except for what I'm here to do.

"Talk to me, Arden," Locke's voice crackles in my ear, low and steady. His tone isn't worried yet, but it's close. "He's moving toward you."

"I see him," I whisper, keeping my smile glued in place. I reach for my drink, pretending to be absorbed in the game. "Relax, Locke. You'll give us away."

"I'll relax when you're back home," he mutters, his voice a rough edge that reveals just how much he hates this. I hide my smirk behind the rim of my glass. He worries too much.

Luke strolls right up to the table, the scent of liquor radiating from him, and takes a seat in the empty chair next to me. "Hey, stranger. Where's your guard dog tonight?"

I turn, meeting his gaze, and the cocky smirk plastered on his face. My brow furrows as I take him in. Up close, in this light, he's not even handsome. He just looks expensive.

Tailored suit, diamond cufflinks, the faint gloss of sweat at his temple, and a million-dollar smile. Underneath it all, he has another look that I know all too well. The hollow, frantic glow of a man chasing something he'll never catch. The look of an addict. And judging by the way he's standing here, eyeing me, he doesn't have just one vice.

"Excuse me?" I tilt my head, letting confusion lace my words as I give him a slow once-over. Whatever magic or charm he has on screen, it doesn't follow him off set.

"Locke," he says, leaning back in his chair. "I saw you two at the gala, remember? And my party." He looks at me expectantly, his brow furrowed in a way that says he's waiting for me to remember, but he keeps talking. "You're not fooling anyone, you know. The way he looked at you? Like he was ready to kill me just for breathing in your direction."

Well, well, well... Even with all that alcohol in his system, his memory is crystal clear. I laugh lightly, swirling my drink. "We're not together," I say with a practiced edge that suggests he's a distant memory, "and he's certainly not here."

Then, I see something else take over his expression. Dark isn't even the word. This look is absolutely menacing. It might have made me flinch at one point, before I learned better. I don't flinch now. I let a smile spread slowly over my lips and tilt my head toward the blackjack table.

"Want to play?" I keep my voice light, even as the adrenaline sharpens my focus to a razor's edge.

He studies me for a long moment, then nods and pushes a small stack of chips toward the dealer. "Of course."

The dealer slides two cards to each of us. I flip mine over: a seven and a queen. Seventeen. Decent, but not perfect. I glance sideways. Luke's eyes are on me, not his cards. Always on me.

He turns over a six and a ten. Sixteen. He hits, but the jack sends him over the edge to twenty-six. Bust.

"Tough luck," I say lightly, waving a hand to stay with my seventeen.

The dealer flips her last card: a nine. She busts too. My pile of chips doubles as the winnings are pushed my way.

Luke's grin falters for just a second, the tell of a man who's not used to losing. He drums his fingers against the table. "I guess tonight's your lucky night," he says. His voice is quiet and threaded with something poisonous.

"Maybe." I meet his gaze again; his eyes look almost black.

He smiles, but it's hollow. There's something hungry in his gaze, a calculated interest that makes my stomach twist. Maybe it's because I already know what kind of man he is, maybe it's just the anticipation.

I keep my focus on the game, watching the dealer slide another hand across the felt. Every sound fades except for the soft snap of the cards and the rhythmic tap of Luke's ring against the table.

He wins the round by a hair, closing the distance between us until I'm breathing in the scent of his cologne. "You're good," he says, voice dropping to a near whisper. "Too good for someone just out here having fun."

I offer him a practiced smile. "I like to win."

His grin is sharp. "I know the feeling."

"Let's make things a little more interesting," he says, pushing a larger stack of chips forward. "Loser buys the next round?"

I meet his challenge with a smirk. "Sure. But, like I said, I don't lose."

He chuckles. It's a dark sound, and for a moment, the mask slips. I catch a flash of something vindictive beneath the charm. He knows I'm baiting him, and I get the feeling that he doesn't enjoy being played with.

The next hand is quick. I pull a king and an ace. Blackjack. His smile falters, but he covers it with a swallow of his drink.

"Well," I say, my voice steady and laced with just enough charm to keep him hooked, "I guess the next one's on you." I lift my nearly empty glass for him to see.

Luke stands, downing what's left of the drink in his glass, eyes still fixed on me. "Then let's not waste time. There's a private bar upstairs. Better drinks, because I'm making them."

There it is. The opening. This is the invitation I've been waiting for.

I don't skip a beat, my expression remaining perfectly level as I set my glass down. "Lead the way."

Luke offers me his arm, and I take it, letting him guide me toward the elevator at the back of the lounge. The mirrored doors slide open, reflecting our faces side by side. He's the perfect image of a man who thinks he's won. It's almost funny; he has no idea I'm just getting started.

We step in, and the doors close. Game on.

Chapter 32
LOCKE

My eyes stay glued to the screens in front of Tiernan and me from the moment I notice him get up from that table and cut across the room. Luke Holloway. Sauntering over to her like he owns this casino and everything in it.

The kind of swagger that screams trouble and expensive grooming habits. A smug grin plastered on his face as he boldly strikes up a conversation. I can't even watch him talk to her without wanting to rip his throat out. The rest of the casino is just a static hum on the monitors. A glittering blur of people who think this is just another night. They have no idea that they're sitting next to a monster.

In Hollywood, rumors go around quicker than in a high school hallway, and none of the stories I've heard about Luke are good. Tales of his parties border on urban legend, because no one leaves with proof. Phones are confiscated at the door. There are whispers of underage girls being invited in, used as disposable playthings. Arden was horrified by what she saw, and I don't blame her.

I used to get invited, requested even. That was before Luke made a hobby out of targeting people I love. We've been on opposite sides of the line for too long now.

They sit together, playing blackjack and casually flirting for what seems like an eternity. Watching her go through the motions; smiles, giggles, the little rehearsed tilt of her head. It's supposed to make him think he's in control, but it breaks me in ways I simply refuse to acknowledge right now.

He keeps inching closer. Seeing how far he can get with her in such a public space. He rests his hand on the back of her chair, a casual motion, and waits. She leans in close again, laughing at some corny joke. Perfectly playing the part of a woman who's charmed.

Then, he inches his fingers down to her thigh. My jaw tightens, because I know he won't stop there. Tiernan notices the change in my posture, slowing his typing to study the monitor, but he doesn't speak. There's nothing I'd love more than to go down there and give Luke what he actually deserves. Not smiles and flirty banter, but something much more painful.

Forty-five minutes in, and Luke keeps testing boundaries like a man on credit. He leans in close and whispers something in her ear. Thank fuck for microscopic earpieces and microphones. I hear it perfectly. "Loser buys the next round?" When he pulls back, I see the look he's giving her. His mouth is smiling, but his eyes are hollow. Dead.

Then Arden wins, and I know what's coming before he even opens his mouth. The invitation that'll get her through his door. Luke stands close and extends his arm to her. They move toward the elevator like a picture-perfect couple on a date.

My hands curl around the chairback I'm no longer sitting in. Everything outside this camera feed feels irrelevant; my world narrows to that elevator and the hallway camera, and to the hollow feeling behind my ribs whenever she smiles at him.

She's a pro; she knows how to push men like him just far enough to be irresistible. But "far enough" is a dangerous line, and I measure it through the minor changes in his face: the slackening at his mouth, the hollow in his gaze when he thinks no one sees.

"Watch your back; we're here if you need us." I croak into my mic. They're the first words I've spoken in almost an hour. I know she can't respond, but as they enter the elevator, I notice her shoot a glance at the camera in the corner. The words hang there. Half promise, half warning. Because saying them gives me the illusion of action.

"We'll lose visibility when they get in that room," Tiernan warns me. My heart skips a beat, but I knew this was coming. "The elevator is covered, the hall up to Luke's door is filmed, but beyond that no video feeds." I give him a quick nod.

In the hallway, we have a narrow view of them as they approach Luke's door. The room is thick with the kind of silence that presses in and threatens to suffocate you. Arden finds the camera and gives one more tiny, almost-hidden look before she lets him unlock the door. That small, careful motion steadies me more than I should admit. I tell myself that's enough. I tell myself she knows what she's doing.

Before Luke opens the door, I unclench my jaw just enough to get out the words, "If anything feels off, get out. I'll handle the rest." It's a risk I haven't and wouldn't offer to anyone else.

They disappear into the suite, and every second stretches even further. I let out a breath between trembling lips. I am not built to watch and wait; I'm built to move. But I stay. I sit. I listen to anything I can catch on the other end of my earpiece, the scratch of a chair, a laugh that feels much too light for the occasion.

Tiernan's breath, and continued typing, anchors me like a distant wave. I let the heat pool and burn in my chest until the impulse to go down there and tear everything apart is something I can feel aching in my bones.

The thing about waiting is that it gives you time to think. The longer I don't move, the more certain I become of two truths, one ugly and one stubbornly protective. Ugly: men like Luke get worse when given silence. Protective: Arden is not a thing to be saved; she's a person to be trusted and backed up only when necessary. Both truths hurt.

I turn, staring out the window of our temporary headquarters. Struggling to catch every crackling word Arden speaks. Just to make sure she's okay. I'm just a man doing my best to guard what I swore I'd protect, even as fear claws at me, urging me to put an end to the whole job right here. But if the worst of my nightmares comes out to play, walking away won't be an option for either of us. He made the mistake of thinking she was just another trophy; I'll make sure it's the last mistake he ever makes.

Chapter 33
ARDEN

Walking into the suite, I almost can't believe my eyes. Even Locke's wasn't this extravagant. I can see why these are set aside for the most elite players. I stop just inside the doorway to take in the view. Unfortunately, the floor-to-ceiling windows aren't what catch my attention first. Sienna Vale sits perched on the curved leather couch, a light pink cocktail in hand and a look of pure venom on her face.

"Luke, honey," she purrs, her eyes raking over my red lace dress with practiced disdain. "I thought we agreed on no strays tonight."

Luke chuckles, heading toward the bar. "Don't be jealous, Sienna. I'm sure you remember Locke's little shadow from the gala." He turns to me again. "Arden, was it?"

My pulse throbs, but I keep my expression a smooth, unfazed mask. "It's really a small town, Sienna," I say, sliding onto a barstool at the far end of the bar, away from her. "It's hard not to bump into familiar faces."

I do my best to case the suite without looking too suspicious. I don't know why I bother, honestly; there are no emergency exits. There's a balcony, but jumping would be a death sentence. I see hallways on either side of me that lead to more rooms, but the only way out is the door we just walked through.

The most interesting part of this place is a human-sized birdcage with a swing inside, sitting front and center. Part of me is curious enough to want to sit on it, but I'm not stupid enough to put myself in the position of getting locked in a cage by these two lunatics right now.

I note Luke's laptop sitting on the bar, still open from whatever he was doing before the lounge; he's making this far too easy.

"Sienna, why don't you go get some air," Luke orders, his voice dismissive and cold as he prepares our drinks. She huffs, rolls her eyes dramatically, and disappears through the glass doors. I'm not wasting any time.

I slip a small USB drive from inside my bra and quickly plug it into the side of his laptop. I listen as the low hum of the fan stops. Tiernan said that would happen if it worked. At least that's covered.

"So..." I start, trying to sound like I didn't just fry his computer. "You must stay here often if they just *gave* you this room."

"Yeah, Vegas is basically my second home. I know gambling isn't the best habit, but I'm good at it and it fills the time when I'm not working."

I nod as he glances over his shoulder at me. "That makes sense," I respond. "I can see why you'd want to come to a place like Vegas. So full of people and parties, it must be easier to blend in, right? Everyone's so focused on having a good time that they probably don't even notice you."

He pauses, his hands cutting an orange into thin slices as he contemplates. "Yeah," he finally mutters. "It also beats sitting in a mansion in L.A.... alone." He mixes vodka and some ingredients I don't recognize together in a stainless-steel shaker. "Fame can be lonely, you know?" he adds as he shakes the mixture over his right shoulder.

My head tilts, and I gaze toward the balcony, where Sienna's silhouette is stark against the bright neon lights. "I find that hard to believe." I reply, my voice dripping with feigned sympathy. "You have Sienna right there."

Luke pauses, his eyes cutting to mine with a flicker of something vicious. "This thing with Sienna isn't real. She's nice to look at, the sex is great, but let's be honest — she isn't exactly interesting. She's just part of the brand." He shrugs, totally dismissive of the woman who's standing twenty feet away.

Aw, the rich and famous actor wants me to feel bad for him. I didn't think he could get any more pathetic, but somehow, he keeps proving me wrong. He isn't just a narcissist, or just an asshole; he's a predator who doesn't even view his own girlfriend as a person. He views her simply as an asset.

Luke turns around again, pouring liquid into two glasses, and I take this opportunity to remove the USB I plugged into his computer

Each glass has an orange slice floating on top of the pinkish liquid and a tiny straw inside. He offers me the glass in his left hand, drinks from the one in his right, and then sits down next to me, watching me the entire time. I put the straw in my mouth and pretend to take a sip, but I'm not that stupid. I know what he's capable of.

In an effort to get the drink out of my hand, I reach for my phone, mustering up as much feigned enthusiasm as I can manage. Then I sing out, "Hey, let's take a selfie! It's not every day you're in Luke Holloway's penthouse."

He sets his drink down next to mine, chuckling and nodding in agreement. Leaning in, he wraps an arm around my waist, sliding his hand along my lower back on the way. My skin is crawling, especially after his comments about Sienna, but I fight the urge to pull away.

I take the photo quickly and look back down at the screen. "I can AirDrop it to you, or are you one of those green-text-bubble guys?"

Luke lets out another small chuckle. "Yeah, I'll take it. Maybe I'll show Locke the next time I run into him. I'd love to see the look on his face when he finds out we were alone together."

I swallow down a cackle at the thought of just how much Locke already knows and settle for a shallow, mindless giggle instead. "Luke's iPhone? It's on the way!"

I watch as he taps on the screen to accept the file with a smug, unsuspecting grin on his face. He's so blinded by his own ego that he doesn't even realize he just invited a malicious payload directly onto his phone. He thinks he's getting ammo he can use against Locke. In reality, he just handed Tiernan the keys to his whole digital life.

"Nice moves, A. I'm in," I hear Tiernan whisper through my earpiece. "Keep him occupied a bit longer, will you?"

I let out a sigh of relief and grab my drink from the bar top. It feels like the hard part is over. Now I wait. Luke sips from his glass, while I consider my next move.

Just then, the glass door slides open, and Sienna saunters back in from the balcony. She doesn't look refreshed; she looks bored and eager to start trouble. She stops by the bar, trailing a perfectly manicured finger over the back of Luke's neck before her eyes lock onto mine.

"Still here?" she asks, her voice dripping with sheer disgust. "I thought you'd have bored him to death by now."

I don't want to drink, but with both of them staring at me like I'm the evening's entertainment, it's getting harder to avoid. I take a small sip. It tastes fine, smells fine too, but I know that means nothing. If they drugged this, they'll be waiting for the first slip.

"Hey, did you see that giant birdcage?" I ask, looking around the space to break the tension.

"Of course, how could anyone miss it?" Luke says, rolling his eyes. They're glazing over in a way that wasn't there before; the alcohol must be catching up to him.

"It's hideous, isn't it?" Sienna adds with a bitter smirk on her lips. She leans against the bar, watching me over the rim of her glass. "Luke was throwing a total fit because someone snagged his usual suite tonight. He thinks this one is *gaudy*."

She pauses, her eyes raking over me with practiced disdain before she lets out a sharp, mocking laugh.

"I told him I'd happily let him lock me in there just to make the decor worth it, but he wasn't interested." Her smile sharpens as she looks me up and down. "Maybe he's looking for something a little more unwilling tonight. Is that it?"

"What, you don't like it?" I ask Luke, ignoring Sienna and trying to sound fascinated while I slowly start making my way over to the gold bars, drawing him away from the bar and her watchful eyes.

Luke doesn't look at Sienna or acknowledge her comment. He just huffs, his words thick and slurring as he focuses entirely on me. "It *is* gaudy. Cheap gimmicks for people with no taste. Like she said, some asshole snagged my favorite penthouse tonight, so I'm stuck with it."

He takes a heavy swallow of his drink, his eyes dark and body swaying. As he says it, a spark of satisfaction flares in my chest. I can't help but wonder if Locke is the one sitting in his favorite room right now.

As I approach the cage, I stare at the golden bars as if I'm admiring a piece of historic art. Luke follows behind me, still swaying. Sienna is a few steps behind him, like a handler watching her animal move in for the kill.

Every step they take makes my heart rate spike. He's staring at me with that sinister look in his eyes again. I keep waiting to feel something. The drugs or adrenaline, relief, or even fear. But I don't feel anything.

I'm not *afraid* of Luke, and I'm definitely not intimidated by Sienna's attempts to act the part of a villainous sidekick. Giving them what they deserve is going to be the most satisfying thing I've ever done. I just need Tiernan to give me my cue to leave.

He catches up to me near the cage, wobbling even as he stands still. Sienna stands just behind his shoulder, her arms crossed, looking at me in a way that makes me feel like I'm trapped *inside* the cage.

"Can you tell me why you're so obsessed with this thing?" His voice slurs, pale lips barely able to form the words. I stare at him, straining to gauge how much he's actually had to drink today.

"Oh, I don't know," I say, shooting a look at Sienna before landing back on Luke with a wink. "Maybe I want you to lock me in it, like she said. Are you into that?"

Sienna's eyes flash with a dark, twisted spark of excitement. "Careful what you wish for, sweetheart," she purrs.

He squints at me through whatever haze the drinking has put him in, then lets out a breathy laugh. "You're insane."

"Maybe." I shrug, keeping the smile. "But aren't you curious?"

He shifts, coming in close enough for his lips to graze the outer edge of my ear as he whispers, "I'm more curious about what's hiding under your little dress." He slips a finger under the strap, letting it snap back into place, as he says it.

My body freezes. I hold his gaze, but my mind is racing. His balance is off, his words are slow... he's different from what he was even a few minutes ago. I give him a weak smile. His eyelids grow heavier, and the way he keeps looking at me sets my nerves on edge. What the hell did he drink?

And then it comes crashing in on me. Oh, God, he isn't just tipsy. He drugged himself. That explains the sluggish grin, the heavy eyelids, the slurring.

A wicked thrill runs through me, and I bite back yet another bout of laughter fighting its way up my throat, barely keeping it contained. A victorious smile spreads across my face instead as I stare into his glassy eyes.

He notices instantly. "Oh, you like that?"

"Oh, Luke," I whisper as he leans into me, the bars of the cage cold against my back. "I don't think you know what you've gotten yourself into."

He licks his lips, pure hunger flickering in his eyes as he trails a finger from the strap of my dress down to my cleavage. "Oh, I think you're right. How about you show me?" he slurs, swaying forward.

His weight presses me further into the cage, the bars digging into my spine. My breath catches. He's too close, too heavy. Every inch of him reeks of arrogance and that musky cologne. *Maybe this isn't my winning move after all.*

I brace my hands against his chest, pushing him back slightly, running a finger down the buttons on his shirt. Pretending it's a game, but in reality, I'm steadying him. Keeping him just far enough away that I still have some control.

"I knew you'd come around, darling," he slurs, his eyelids heavy, but his gaze is still glued to mine.

I steal a glance at the clock on the wall, counting down the seconds until whatever he put in that drink finally knocks him out. But it's not happening. Five seconds pass. Ten. Panic floods my chest as his weight continues to press in on me. His breath hot on my neck and his hands inching lower down my sides.

I look past his shoulder, hoping to see Sienna concerned, but she's standing there watching the struggle with a faint look of amusement.

"Don't hold your breath for him to take a nap," she mutters, swirling her glass. "Luke has a tolerance that would kill a normal man. Whatever was in that... it's only going to make him mean."

My heart drops. *She knows.* She's been watching the whole time, enjoying the slow-motion train wreck.

I clear my throat, trying to regain my footing. "Let's—" I manage, but before I can get another word out, Luke's mouth is on my neck, and his grip tightens violently on my hips. His fingertips dig into my skin hard enough to make me gasp.

He glances up, grinning, teeth bared. "Are you sure you knew what *you* were getting yourself into?

Once again, my body feels frozen. All of his weight presses me harder against the metal, and my spine is screaming for relief.

No... not again. The whisper in the back of my mind is small, terrified, and dangerously close to breaking me. I'm staring at Luke, but for a split second, I'm seeing a ghost from a memory I thought was long gone.

"Luke, stop. This hurts," I whisper, the panic finally clawing at the back of my throat.

I look at Sienna one last time, pleading silently for a shred of womanly solidarity, but she just tilts her head and takes a slow, mocking sip of her drink. She isn't going to help. She's waiting for the real show to start.

Luke places one finger over my lips, signaling me to stop talking. His eyes are nearly black as his mouth continues its trail past my collarbone.

I'm working to bring my knee up when the suite door doesn't just open, it's nearly thrown off its hinges.

Locke is there, and he looks nothing like the polished man he usually presents himself as. He looks like a storm wearing a dark suit and made of pure, unadulterated rage. Behind him, Tiernan slips into the room, holding a tablet and looking entirely too calm to be here.

Locke is across the room in one blurry heartbeat. He doesn't shout. He doesn't warn. He just reaches out, grabs the back of Luke's collar and his belt, and rips him off me with such violent force that Luke's feet actually leave the ground.

Locke flings him toward the center of the room, not even looking to see where he lands. At that moment, time seems to stand still.

I watch as Luke stumbles backward, his sluggish balance finally failing him as he crashes over the back of the leather couch. He grasps for a floor lamp on the way down, and it shatters against the tile in a million tiny pieces.

A sick, wet cracking sound reverberates through the suite as his head meets the edge of the coffee table. Then, there's only silence.

I stand by the cage, eyes wide and chest heaving, my eyes pressed on Locke's back. His shoulders are rising and falling with heavy, jagged breaths. He doesn't look at me, not yet. He walks straight to where Luke is lying on the floor, motionless among the glass shards, and stares down at him.

Sienna finally breaks. The glass slips from her hand, shattering on the marble bar. "Oh my God," she gasps, her face turning a ghostly shade of white as she looks at Luke's crumpled form. "You... you killed him. You fucking killed him!"

Locke turns slowly to look at her. His expression revealing nothing but a lethal indifference that makes her scream die in her throat. He doesn't look like a man who just committed a crime; he looks like a man who just finished a chore.

"And you're a witness," he says, his voice a low, terrifying rumble that vibrates through the suite.

Sienna stumbles back, her hands and voice shaking. "I'll tell the police. I'll tell everyone! I have the platform, I have —"

"You have nothing, Sienna," Tiernan interrupts, tapping his screen and turning the tablet toward her. "I've spent the last ten minutes downloading the 'Inventory' folder from Luke's cloud. You know, the one with the photos of the girls you helped him lure and traffic? The wire transfers you signed to pay off their families? If the police come in here, they're going to find a dead predator and a mountain of evidence pointing to *you* as his primary accomplice."

I watch as Locke looms over her, and I take a moment to study the face of the woman who found my struggle so amusing just moments ago. There's no mockery left in her expression. In its place is a raw fear that makes her look smaller. The mask has shattered, leaving nothing behind but a terrified girl who realized too late that she's been playing the wrong game.

Locke continues. "We've already drafted the narrative, Sienna. We have the messages, we have the photos, and we have the motive. If you say a single word, we won't just ruin your career. We'll make sure you spend the rest of your life in a cell, since Luke can't."

Sienna looks at Luke's body, then back at Locke's cold, unwavering gaze. The animosity is gone, replaced by the frantic, pathetic survival instinct of a cornered animal. She looks like she might even faint. "I just did what he told me!"

"Get out," Locke orders. He doesn't shout, and the smooth, calm tone of his voice is even more unnerving. "Get out of this city. Get out of this country. If I ever see your face on a screen or hear your name mentioned in Hollywood again, he will hit send on that file. Do you understand?"

Sienna doesn't wait to be told twice. She grabs her clutch off a nearby chair and bolts, her heels clicking frantically against the tile until the door slams shut behind her.

Locke finally turns to me. The hardness in his eyes softens, just a fraction. He reaches out, his thumb brushing my cheek.

"You're okay," he says, and for the first time tonight, I actually believe it.

Chapter 34
LOCKE

The second I heard her voice through the mic, panicked and pleading with him to stop, the world turned red. I didn't care about the plan. I didn't care about Jaxon. I only cared about the fact that Luke Holloway's hands were on my woman.

I know she probably hates me for this. For barging in, for not trusting her to handle it. But what else could I do? The part of me that has been waiting to get my hands on Luke all night is extremely satisfied. The other part is a frantic mess, blinded by the need to check for bruises and make sure that none of the blood on the floor belongs to her.

The door slams shut behind Sienna, and finally, the suite is quiet. I don't look at the body on the floor again. I don't care about the mess. My eyes go straight to Arden.

She's still standing by that ridiculous cage, her back pressed against the bars, chest heaving. She looks like a statue, beautiful and terrifyingly still.

"Arden," I rasp. My voice sounds foreign to my own ears, thick with the remnants of a rage I haven't fully extinguished. I'm across the room in a heartbeat. Cupping her face in my hands, my thumbs brushing over her cheekbones. I need to feel her warmth, to prove to myself she's still here and in one piece.

"Are you okay? Did he hurt you? Tell me where he touched you."

Her eyes finally find mine. A sudden, fierce spark of reality replaces the vacant look in her eyes. She's not crumbling. She hasn't cried. She just reaches out, her fingers digging into my forearms as if to steady herself... or me.

"I'm fine," she whispers, though her voice trembles. "You... you killed him. Locke, you actually did that."

"I told you I would take care of it," I mutter, leaning my forehead against hers. I close my eyes for a second, letting the adrenaline start its slow retreat. "No one will ever touch you like that and get away with it. Not when I'm around."

I feel her exhale a breath she's probably been holding since I burst through the door. For a moment, we just stand there in the penthouse's wreckage. Two souls suddenly bound by a secret that would destroy most people.

"Seb's five minutes out." Tiernan's voice breaks the silence. I had almost forgotten he was still standing by the bar, his face illuminated by the blue light of his tablet. He looks completely unfazed as he taps and slides his fingers over the screen, already deconstructing Luke's digital life.

"He's bringing a crew. They'll scrub the suite and ensure the security footage shows Luke entering alone and never leaving. By tomorrow, this will just be a drunken accident with no witnesses."

"And Sienna?" I ask, my eyes still on Arden.

"She's halfway to the parking garage by now," Tiernan replies, a grim smile tugging at his lips. "Terrified, no doubt. She knows that if she breathes a word, that folder will be on its way to the Feds. She'll stay quiet to save her own skin. People like her always do."

I nod, then turned my attention back to Arden. She's looking past me now, at the spot where Luke's blood is dripping and soaking into the white fur rug. The reality of the crime must be setting in.

"Don't look," I command softly, hooking my hand under her chin to pull her gaze back to me. "I don't want you to see any more of this."

Without waiting for her to answer, I scoop her into my arms. Her body relaxes as she tucks her head into the crook of my neck. I can feel the racing beat of her heart against my chest, a frantic rhythm I wish I could soothe on my own.

I walk just a few feet and sit her on the edge of a dining chair. "Tiernan, the kit," I call out. Tiernan reaches deep into his bag and tosses over a sterile pack of antiseptic wipes.

Taking her hands in mine, I carefully wipe away any stray smudge of Luke's DNA from her skin. I clean her knuckles and palms, then move to her neck to wipe away the phantom touch of his mouth.

"Locke," she whispers, her voice breaking as the tears finally fall. "The room... the evidence..."

"It's taken care of, Arden. All of it." I look up, meeting her eyes with a steadiness I don't entirely feel. "Seb's crew will ensure that the only DNA in this room belongs to Luke and Sienna. Your fingerprints, your hair, your presence. It'll all be gone. You were never here. This was just a drunken accident."

I finish cleaning her and take off my suit jacket, draping it over her shoulders. She's swimming in it, but I'm hoping it can offer an ounce of comfort while we're still stuck in this room.

Then, Seb is knocking at the door. I knew he was my best friend and right-hand man for a reason. "Damn, that was quick," I say as he enters the small walkway leading into the penthouse.

He responds with an exaggerated "Damn!" before adding, "this place is nice. Remind me to snag one of these sometime. Just maybe not this one. Don't want to share the space with the ghost of this asshole."

I let out a rough, mirthless laugh, shaking my head. "This way."

"Well, at least you were efficient." Seb nods as he takes stock of the damage. He's not wrong. Sure, there's glass everywhere, but that goes along with the 'accident' narrative we're crafting. The only real mess is the pool of blood that has dripped from this poor bastard's head. "Easy cleanup. I'll get my guys here right away." He shrugs and walks off, taking his phone out of his pocket as he moves into the kitchen.

I turn back to Arden. She's staring at the floor, huddled under my suit jacket as if she's trying to disappear into the fabric.

"Arden," I whisper. She doesn't look up. Just stares at the floor, like if she doesn't make eye contact, none of this is real. Trying to will it away.

I crouch in front of her. "You okay?"

She nods slowly. A reflex. A lie.

I don't push. I just glide a finger down her cheek, trying my best to give her some sense of comfort. "It's over."

When she finally speaks, her voice comes out small. "He's really dead?"

"He is," I say. "He'll never touch you, or anyone else, ever again."

That gets her attention. She finally makes eye contact. Her eyes are bloodshot and searching mine.

"Locke..." she says. "Thank you... for coming for me."

My eyes meet hers, and I unclench my jaw enough to say, "You never have to thank me for that. You call, I come. That's how this works."

I rise to my feet, my voice turning to steel again as Seb's crew slips into the room behind me, moving with the silence of shadows. "Tiernan, clear the service elevator. I'm getting her out of here."

"Path is clear," Tiernan announces, tapping his tablet to loop the hallway cameras one last time. "Go. I'll stay until the crew is finished."

I don't want Arden to see any more of this. The way they'll position Luke's limbs, the way they'll tilt the lamp to make the fall look natural. I scoop her up, keeping her face pressed into my shoulder so she doesn't have to look at the body as we walk past.

As the heavy penthouse door clicks shut behind us, the air in the hallway feels suddenly, violently cold. Time seems to slow down. Luke Holloway's body is still lying there, but he's already becoming a memory.

I walk toward the service elevator, feeling the weight of her in my arms and the secret we now share. By morning, the world will mourn a tragic accident. Only we'll know the truth.

And I can finally turn my attention toward the mess this asshole left behind.

Chapter 35
ARDEN

It's been four days since Locke got me out of that hotel room. Three since I left my bed at all. I should be sleeping. Eating. Grateful I walked out without a scratch. But I can't stop watching it.

The video.

Tiernan sent me a folder full of Luke's cloud files the day after we left the hotel. I asked him to. I thought it might make his death easier to justify. Maybe it has, but at what cost?

Countless hours of his life are now sitting on my phone like a loaded gun. I should have deleted it all.

Instead, I opened every single file.

Some I couldn't finish. Couldn't stomach. Still can't.

Others, I wish I'd left alone.

All of them are the same: Luke's voice. Luke's hands. Girls who can't stand upright. Girls with their eyes half-closed and voices too weak to speak... or scream. Girls who should be in school, not in some rich asshole's hotel room.

He keeps the camera rolling, laughing while he takes advantage of them. And while he hurts them. He treats it like a joke. Like this is his favorite form of entertainment.

He was never going to stop.

And then I found the videos of Jaxon. An entire folder full of memories. Most are harmless, the pair on vacation, or doing silly skits and telling jokes together like best friends do. But there's one Luke kept separate. One that was clearly meant for a different purpose.

It's Jaxon, but his hair is longer, hanging down in his face in a way he never wears it anymore. He's sitting on what looks like a hotel bed, judging by the blankets still covering it. The camera is recording from a few feet away, and the footage is shaky, so someone else was clearly holding it.

He looks toward the camera, and his eyes are completely glazed over. He's swaying, even as he sits there. His shirt was already off when the video started, but he's still wearing black leather pants and combat boots.

Then, someone else stumbles into the frame. A girl who looks like she can't be a day over sixteen. She's still clothed, wearing a simple yellow sundress. Her hair is sticking to her cheek like she's been sweating. Something about her outfit and the way she nearly falls as she takes a step towards the bed makes her look so innocent.

That's the worst part. She looks like me. The 'me' that existed before I learned how to bite back. Before I figured out how to turn my body into a trap instead of falling into someone else's.

Jaxon looks at her, but it's not recognition in his gaze; it's confusion. He blinks slowly and rubs his eyes as if he's trying to focus on what's in front of him. She sinks down on the edge of the bed beside him, her head dropping against his shoulder almost instantly, as though her body can't manage to hold it up anymore. Neither of them speaks. Neither of them even moves. It's like they're frozen.

From behind the camera, Luke's laugh cuts through the silence, sharp, low, and gloating. A familiar sound that makes my skin crawl and stomach turn all over again.

He coaxes in a mocking drawl from behind the lens, "She's cute, Jax. Don't pass out yet, you'll miss all the fun." But neither of them responds.

The girl lifts her head from Jaxon's shoulder slowly, like it takes everything she has just to move. Luke zooms in, the frame tilting sickeningly close to her face.

"Hey sweetie," his voice croons, too soft, too sweet, like poison coated in sugar, "why don't you give him a kiss?"

My stomach drops as the realization sets in. I've seen her.

Not like this, glassy-eyed and hollow. But just last week, on stage at Jaxon's show. A slightly older version, screaming every lyric until her throat went raw. The same girl who gazed at Jaxon like he hung the stars himself. And left with him.

But here she was, younger, drugged, and propped against Jaxon's shoulder like a lifeless doll. Reduced to nothing but a pawn in Luke's game. The video lingers on her face for a moment before panning over to Jaxon's; his eyes fall shut as he collapses onto the mattress. Then it cuts off.

I can't stop hitting play, rewinding, zooming in. Inspecting every inch of the footage, attempting to fill in the blanks. Where were they? When was this? How does he know her? And why did it feel like they shared something real on stage?

The room tilts.

My fingers go numb.

And when I blink, I'm not in my room at all anymore.

I'm eighteen. Sitting in that hallway again.

The carpet is worn thin under my bare feet. The smell of smoke clings to my hoodie. Mom's bedroom door is closed in front of me. The house has been too quiet for too long.

I already knew.

When I finally gathered the courage to go in, she was nearly falling off the bed, the needle still in her arm. Eyes half-open and empty, looking at nothing. Skin as cold as ice.

I couldn't move. Couldn't think. Couldn't do anything. And then *he* was there. Not a friend. Not a neighbor. The man who came when my mom was late on what she owed. The one who took debts in cash... and sometimes other ways, too.

He's leaning in the doorway like he owns the place. Looking at me like he owns me now, too. "You don't belong here, pretty thing," he says. "Let's get you out of this dump."

I thought he meant out of Vegas.

He told me he could introduce me to an agent. That he'd make me a model... and I believed him.

The studio smelled of hairspray and old coffee. There was a pristine white backdrop and lights so bright I couldn't see anything past them.

"One more," they'd say. "Turn your shoulder. Lift your chin. Perfect." They paid me in cash, not much, just enough to make it feel legit.

Then it was, "A little less fabric, you want to get paid, don't you?" I kept telling myself it was normal. This was just how modeling worked. But the paychecks eventually stopped coming.

One day, they booked me a "private shoot" at a hotel suite. No lights, no backdrop. Just a group of men on the couch with drinks in their hands. The oldest one smiled as if he'd just been handed his favorite dessert. He told me to relax, that we'd warm up before the actual shoot.

They took my phone and my bag. Claiming it was "safer" that way. It didn't take long for me to understand what they meant. A younger one brought me champagne, claiming it would help me relax. My lips barely touched it.

The door clicked shut behind me and locked. I laughed it off, kept my face pretty while my gut was screaming at me to run. But I was 10 stories up, and there was nowhere to go.

Then one of them stood up and came in close. His hands were on my arms, then sliding down to my waist. He turned me around as if I were something to inspect. "Perfect," he said. The rest just laughed.

They made me stand against the wall. Told me how to pose and what to take off. They curated every angle. Every move felt like it belonged to them. The photos did, too.

Then, there were fingers on my skin where they didn't belong. The sound of a zipper pulled down. A hand over my mouth when I finally found my voice. Threats to hurt me in other ways if I drew too much attention. The camera never stopped flashing.

It didn't last long. Just long enough to make me understand no one was coming to save me. When it was over, I was a shaking, sobbing mess. I couldn't even look at myself in the mirror. Of course they just left me there. The damage had been done.

I don't remember leaving or how I got to Lexi's house. Just her voice, raw and full of panic, when she opened the door.

Chapter 36
LOCKE

The sound of a piercing scream rips my attention away from the movie on the TV screen. I haven't left the condo since the hotel, nor has Lexi.

We've spent the past four days trying to convince Arden to leave her room, bringing food and water, reminding her we're here to help. She won't talk to either of us, won't even look at us. Zoe managed to sneak in a few times, but Lexi put a stop to it with a single look. She didn't try again. Mothers have a way of doing that.

But when I hear Arden scream, I don't think; I just run. I'm grateful to find the door unlocked, but nothing would stop me from getting into this bedroom even if it wasn't. I find her in bed, wrapped up in blankets, thrashing around like she's trying to fight an invisible person off.

"Arden?" I try to calm my voice as I rush to scoop her into my arms. I wrap them around her tightly, doing my best to contain her until she settles.

After a few minutes, she slowly opens her eyes and stares up at me. She blinks a few times, working to orient herself, and glances around the room. I feel her grip loosen on my arm and her breathing slow to a normal pace. I expect her to push me away or give me one of those smart-ass comments I've actually grown to miss over the past few days, but all that comes out of her mouth is, "Stay?"

"Always," I whisper in return.

I waited in Arden's bed all night, tossing and turning. Trying to stay alert in case she had another nightmare. She didn't. But now it's morning, and I'm hoping this is the start of her finally coming around. Letting us in on what's been going on in her head.

It's 5 a.m., and I can't pretend I'm trying to sleep anymore. Instead, I decide to get out of bed and track down breakfast. It's a Sunday, so Zoe doesn't have school, which means the house will still be quiet for several hours.

I've been around family my whole life. When you grow up with the kind of father I had, you learn that family is everything.

But ours was the kind that sat shoulder to shoulder at Sunday dinners while keeping one eye on the door. The type that hugged you with one arm while weighing how much trouble you might bring them with the other.

Loyalty was currency, affection was leverage, and you never forgot the bill would come due. Each favor bigger and more costly than the last.

This isn't that.

Lexi doesn't make Arden's coffee because she has to keep her in line. She makes it because she knows exactly how Arden likes it, and because she wants to.

Zoe can get away with sneaking crayons and paper into Arden's room in the middle of the night, and instead of scolding her, Arden lets her stay. Sometimes she even laughs as she cuddles her close.

They move around each other in the kitchen as if they've rehearsed it for years. No jockeying for position, no silent battles for dominance. Just a rhythm they all seem to know. Even the arguments don't carry weight; nobody keeps score.

I've been telling myself I only notice because I've been stuck here too long. Too much downtime makes you study people. But the truth is, I keep finding excuses to watch. To be in the same room as people who claim to love each other unconditionally and actually mean it.

So, I guess that's why I'm out at five in the morning tracking down the best donuts in town. Not because I have to. Not because it's earning me anything. Just because Zoe likes the ones with sprinkles, Lexi always goes for jelly-filled, and Arden... she'll take whatever I hand her without complaint. And because, for reasons I don't want to think too hard about, I want them to wake up to something good.

I enter the loft, placing the large pink box on the kitchen island. There are still no signs of movement in the house. Just the light blue hue that lets me know the sun is slowly making its appearance.

I move toward the coffee machine, starting a pot and reminding myself to order them an espresso machine. This old Mr. Coffee simply isn't cutting it.

When I turn around, I almost jump out of my skin. Arden is standing near the island. She's out of her room, finally. Eyeing the box on the counter, she asks, "How'd you know about this place?" The words come out in a soft tone I don't recall ever hearing from her.

"I remembered you and Lexi talking about it," I shrug. She gives me a weak smile and lifts the lid, peering inside. Her smile grows wider as she notices the chocolate-frosted, Boston cream-filled donut. *Favorite noted.*

She takes one out and places it on the island before approaching me. She stays silent as she wraps her arms around my waist and holds tight for a moment. I let out a sigh of relief as I squeeze her against me.

We could stay like this forever, never saying a word, and I would be satisfied. I pull away slightly, keeping my hands on her hips as I whisper, "Don't you ever do that to me again. Don't lock yourself away and make me wonder if I'll lose you, or already have."

Her breath hitches, a sound so fragile it's hard to believe it belongs to her. For a moment, she just stares at me, wide-eyed, like she doesn't recognize the man in front of her. Then her fingers twist into my shirt, clinging like it's the only thing keeping her steady.

"I thought I was losing myself," she whispers, voice breaking. "I didn't think anyone would notice if I disappeared. But you —" She shakes her head, tears slipping down her cheeks. "You make it impossible to stay lost."

"You don't get it, Arden." I drag a hand down my face, exhaling through my nose. "I've looked down the barrel of a gun and felt nothing. But I came apart the second I thought I might never hear your voice again." The words come out rougher than I mean them to, but my eyes stay locked on hers.

"I don't know how to do this. I don't have all the right words, but I know that there is no world for me without you in it. I'd burn down every city, my business, everything I've ever known, if that's what it took to keep you with me." My fingers curl, tightening my grip on her hips, and I lean forward until my forehead touches hers.

"You think I want money, power, or even freedom? No. The only thing I want is you. If you disappear, I swear to God, I'll disappear with you."

I wrap my arms tightly around her again until she's pushing against me to let go. I ease my grip and give her space to sit at the island. As she takes the first bite of her donut, I pour her a fresh, oversized mug of coffee.

Lexi clued me in to exactly how she likes it. I can finally say we've become friends over the past few days. It's strange how love can pull people together who would never have been in the same room otherwise.

I pull out a barstool and sit next to Arden, simply enjoying being in her presence as golden streaks of light creep over the living room. The only thing that could improve this moment would be a cigar, but there's a strict no-smoking policy in the condo. I guess kids and smoke don't mix.

When she finishes her breakfast, Arden turns to me, still holding her coffee mug with a spark reignited in those big blue eyes.

Her voice is still coarse, but steadier now. "No more shutting you out. No more hiding. Men like Luke never lose... not really. Hollywood is already mourning him, turning him into some kind of golden boy."

She pauses, holding my gaze. "I won't let that lie live on. You want me, Locke? Then you get all of me. And the first thing we're doing is burning that dead son of a bitch's reputation to the ground."

Chapter 37
ARDEN

Ever since that first night, Locke has been nothing like I expected. The past 24 hours have only proven that. I didn't expect those memories to drag me down so deep it felt like I was really back there. I didn't expect to wake up screaming in my bed. And I sure as hell did not expect the view of his stubble, speckled with grey, and those golden-brown eyes staring down at me.

He didn't ask questions, didn't try to fix it; he just stayed.

I didn't expect to want him to, but the way his arms wrapped around me felt like he was shielding me from the world and every bad thing in it.

I've spent years keeping people at arm's length, convincing myself I didn't need anyone else to feel safe. When I told him what I planned to do to Luke Holloway's image and he didn't flinch, didn't talk me out of it, something settled into place. He didn't look at me like I was reckless or broken. He looked as if he understood.

That was enough to make me certain of one thing: he's not going anywhere. It may be too early to call it forever, but for now, he's mine. I'm his.

So, we spent the entire morning planning. Every detail laid out between sips of coffee, right at the kitchen counter. Not just what we'll release, but how. What gets shown and what stays buried.

We'll piece together his worst moments. The ones he thought would never see the light of day. We'll blur every face except his, leaving no room for denial.

Tiernan will handle the distribution. He'll push it to every press outlet, gossip site, and magazine that ever praised the actor, all at once. Leaving no trace of who sent it.

Hollywood is in mourning. Performative candlelight services. Tearful tributes. A whole legacy polished clean by death.

We're going to reverse that narrative.

I can already see the headlines, the hashtags, the chaos. #LukeUncensored. #HollowayExposed. #LukeLeaks. I might even help them along. Let the world finally meet the man they're grieving.

I'm running on caffeine, sugar, and something sharper than adrenaline. Purpose, maybe? Or spite. Either way, it keeps my hands steady as I open my laptop and pull up the editing software before I have time to second-guess myself.

The files load one by one. Luke's face fills the screen, frozen mid-smile. The kind people used to call charming. Looks more like pure evil to me.

Locke stays close, leaning against the counter with his arms crossed, giving me space but never leaving. He doesn't ask what footage I'm using. Doesn't warn me to slow down. He doesn't push for control or soften the edges of what we're about to do. He just watches, present and grounded, like he's ready to catch me if I stumble, but trusting that I won't.

We work for hours.

Cutting. Splicing. Muting audio where it doesn't belong. I make sure Luke is unmistakable in every frame possible. His voice. His laugh. The way he looks at the camera, like he's untouchable. I leave no room for doubt. No excuses. No plausible deniability.

There are moments when my chest tightens, when the familiar burn of nausea crawls up my throat. Scenes I've already seen but still don't want to linger on. But this time, I don't spiral. I don't shut down. I don't look away.

I control the footage now.

What once felt like a loaded gun pressed to my chest has become something else entirely. I get to decide what the world sees and what stays buried. I'm the one holding the gun now.

At some point, Locke glances over at me, his expression searching. I meet his gaze and give him a small nod. A promise, maybe. I'm still here. I'm not breaking.

The sun drifts lower outside the windows, painting the kitchen in warm light that feels at odds with what's playing on my screen. When I finally lean back in my chair, my shoulders ache and my eyes burn, but the montage is complete.

It isn't a highlight reel. It's an unmasking.

```
Subject: Hard Launch
Body: Consider this his
last performance.
Lights, camera, action!
```

I let the cursor hover over the send button for a moment. I know this is the point of no return. Sucking in a deep breath, I click it.

Luke Holloway is already dead, but his image is still alive and well. His name is still protecting the people who enabled him. Still teaching the world that men like him get remembered kindly if they disappear at the right time.

I refuse to let that be the story.

Chapter 38
LOCKE

She's smiling again. Not a smile that looks happy or even relieved. A sharp, dangerous one, like she's daring the world to take another swing at her.

I should focus on the risks. The digital trail we could leave behind, the enemies this could stir up. The way men like Luke always seem to have rot oozing from them, even from beyond the grave.

I don't see any of it. All I can really see is her. That fire in her eyes. The one that dimmed, day by day, until I thought it might be gone for good.

If this goes sideways, I already know the outcome. I'm going down with her.

Maybe that should scare me a little more than it does.

Tiernan's already moving in the background, stacking layers upon layers of distance between us and this mess. By the time the story breaks, the only thing anyone will see is Luke's name going up in flames.

Still, there's really no such thing as a clean break when you're dragging truths like this into the light.

It's almost anticlimactic. The way Arden hits send and closes her laptop like she's clocking out for the day. No real hesitation. No shaky breaths or trembling fingers.

That's when the realization settles in.

Luke Holloway didn't get justice when he died. He got immortalized. His sins got polished away by grief and money and the kind of silence people confuse for respect. This isn't about revenge. It's about refusing to let the lies live longer than he did.

Her smile, the first real one in days, cuts through me like a blade. She stands up, looking at me as if she's asking me to follow her into whatever comes next. I should move, but I'm frozen, overwhelmed by the brutal realization that somewhere between planning sessions, nightmares, and watching her come apart, I fell in love with her. Not despite her history. Not because of what she's done. But because she survived it all.

By the time my brain catches up to my body, I find myself halfway across the room. My hand coils in her hair, tugging her head back just enough to see those blue eyes flare, alive in a way that could bring me to my knees.

"You think you can set the world on fire and just walk away from me?" I say, my voice thick with something I can't even name. "Not a chance."

She doesn't flinch. Doesn't try to hide. She smiles, that same twisted grin, and pulls me down to her mouth like she's been starving. The kiss is all clashing teeth and heat and years of fury burning down to this one moment. She tastes like coffee, sugar, and something absolutely feral. I know this is a hunger I'll never outrun.

When I slam her back against the wall, she giggles against my mouth, a wild, breathless sound. Fuck, it's the most beautiful thing I've ever heard, and it tears me apart. Days of silence, of watching her slip away piece by piece, and now she's here. Alive and burning in my arms.

I pull her tighter against me, grinding her back against the wall until she gasps. My hands roam her body like I've been starving, because I have. I take every curve and every breath as if they belong to me. She fists my shirt, yanking me closer, proving she's just as desperate.

"You don't know what you do to me," I rasp against her throat, teeth grazing her skin before I bite down just hard enough to make her whimper. "Fuck, Arden. There's no way I'm ever letting you go."

Her legs wrap around my waist, locking me in place. Our mouths crash together again, frantic and desperate. Her nails rake down my shoulders, sharp enough to sting, and it only drives me deeper.

I tear her shirt over her head, needing her bare, needing proof she's real and here. Her bra hits the floor a heartbeat later, and I drag my mouth down her chest, tasting, biting, devouring every inch of her skin. It's as if she's the only thing anchoring me in this moment.

She's moaning my name now, head thrown back, spine arched against me, and I swear I could die here and be happy. My fingers work at her leggings, shoving them down, and she kicks free like she's been waiting for this just as long as I have.

"Locke," she gasps, breath hitching as I drag my hand between her thighs, teasing just enough to make her shake. "Don't make me wait."

I grin against her skin, ravenous for her touch. "But you've got no idea how long I already have." She gives me a feral grin and grabs my waist.

I'm inside her in one hard thrust, and everything else disappears. The world goes still. We're the only people who exist. She clutches at me, her grip tightening, pulling me deeper, harder. Every moment is a claim, every sound a surrender. It's chaos and fury and something dangerously close to love, all tangled together.

We come apart in each other's arms, mouths crashing together as if we're afraid to let go. She's laughing against my lips again, breathless and radiant.

Outside, the sun is sinking, flooding the room with gold as if nothing has changed. Even though I know everything has.

The truth is out. The lie is bleeding. And whatever comes next — the headlines, the fallout — I know one thing with brutal clarity.

If the world burns down around us, I'll still be here.

Not because I think we'll survive it.

Because she's worth it all.

Chapter 39

ARDEN

The city doesn't sleep after something like this. It just hums louder, shines brighter, like it's feeding on the chaos.

Inside the loft, the noise feels just as relentless. Phones light up on every available surface, TV screens flicker with headlines and half-formed takes, notifications stack faster than I can process them. I don't touch any of it. I already know what they'll say and, worse, what they'll argue about.

I don't need to scroll to know the internet is doing what it always does when it senses blood in the water. Videos are slowed down and dissected frame by frame. Influencers rushing to weigh in with their newly urgent opinions. Some of them furious. Some of them thoughtful. Some, nauseatingly enough, coming to Luke's defense.

I stand at the window, arms folded tight across my chest, watching the glow of headlights smear across the street below. They stretch and blur together, a restless stream that mirrors the thoughts I can't seem to quiet.

With careful steps, Locke comes up behind me, handling the space around me as if I were breakable. There's no rush in his movements, no assumption that I'll want to be touched, just patience. When his hands settle on my hips, I lean back into him without thinking. The tension in my shoulders eases a bit. I'm tired in a way sleep won't fix, and his presence is the only thing steadying me right now. It reminds me that I'm still here, still breathing, still held.

"That's it," I murmur.

"That's it," he says, quietly validating my statement.

I thought the moment the footage went live would feel different. I thought there would be relief, or triumph, or something that resembled victory. But it just feels like something heavy has finally landed where it was always meant to go. The truth is out. What the world does with it isn't for me to control.

"They're not going to let this go," I say after a moment.

He doesn't pretend otherwise. "No, they probably won't."

I already knew that. Men like Luke don't operate alone. There were handlers. Managers. People who laughed things off because it was easier than asking questions. People who benefited from silence. I didn't just pull one thread; I yanked hard on a tapestry that was never designed to unravel.

Still, I'd do it again.

I tilt my head, resting my temple against Locke's shoulder. "You still think it was worth it?"

"Yes," he says immediately. No doubt in sight.

The certainty in his voice hits me harder than I expected. Something tight and aching in my chest loosens, just a little. I didn't realize how badly I needed that answer until he said it.

Outside, a motorcycle cuts through the traffic below, the sound rising just enough to snag my attention before fading again. Locke's body twitches behind me. It's subtle, the kind of reaction most people wouldn't catch, but I feel it immediately. I glance up at him, but his expression is already smooth and unreadable again.

I decide to let it go. I have enough questions spinning in my head without adding another.

"You okay?" he asks, pressing a kiss to my temple.

I nod. "Just tired."

"Come sit."

He takes my hand and leads me to the couch, where I curl instinctively into his chest; it's muscle memory already. The TV is on but muted, headlines flashing across the screen in bold, urgent fonts. Holloway. Allegations. Unverified footage. Sources say.

Even now, I can see the story being reshaped in real time. Sanded down. Softened. Made more palatable.

After all, no one likes to hear that their favorite celebrity has been a violent predator all this time.

"I keep waiting for the other shoe to drop," I whisper.

"It might," Locke says, his thumb moving in slow, steady strokes along my arm.

I reach for his hand without looking, threading my fingers through his like it will somehow tie us together.

"Promise me something?" I say.

"What is it?" Locke asks, concern taking over his features now.

"Just, if this blows back on us, we'll handle it together. As a team."

"Of course, Arden. Always." He states it as if it were never a question in his mind.

I believe him, even knowing how risky this seems for both of us. Distance has always been how we survived. Letting each other get this close, especially now, feels like lowering every defense when they might still be necessary. The fact that we're still here, still choosing it, means more than any promise.

I can feel my eyelids drooping as I stare at the silent TV screen, exhaustion finally taking over.

At some point, Lexi joins us on the far end of the couch after Zoe's asleep. She curls beneath a blanket, phone loose in her hand, gaze unfocused. She's been like this since I came out of my room, present but not really *here*. Smiling when expected to. Laughing a second too late.

Something is weighing on her. I can feel it. I just wish I had the energy to ask.

The city keeps moving. Sirens wail somewhere in the distance. Wind rattles the windows. And once again, that same low motorcycle engine sound rolls past beneath us.

Locke doesn't react this time. Or maybe he does and I'm just too tired to notice. His phone vibrates on the coffee table as I'm still contemplating.

I feel him still before he says anything. I watch as he scans the screen silently. Then another message comes in, the phone vibrating in his hand. He doesn't show me. He just sets the phone face down on the coffee table again, not even sending a response.

"What was that?" I ask softly.

"Nate. He was checking in," he says after a pause. "Said he can't talk now, though."

That alone is enough to send a ripple of unease through me. I resist the urge to push for more details. I don't think he has any, and whatever's happening there isn't mine to untangle... not yet.

I shift closer to Locke, my fingers sliding under his shirt so I can wrap my arm tighter around him. He tightens his arm around me, too, grounding us both. For the first time since I hit send, I let myself acknowledge what I've been avoiding.

This isn't over.

It might never blow back on us the way I fear. Tiernan did his job. We were careful. This could be the end of it: noise, outrage, speculation, and only the footage to speak for itself.

Or it could spiral into something bigger and darker.

I don't know.

All I know is that I made a choice. I set something in motion. Now I have to live with the aftermath, whatever it might be.

Right now, though, I'm here with the only people I love in this world. Awake enough to know that whatever comes next, I won't face it alone.

That has to be enough, at least for tonight.

Chapter 40

LOCKE

Silence doesn't always mean nothing is happening. Sometimes, it just means you've gotten better at blocking out the noise. Making it wait.

The loft is dark except for the city bleeding in through the windows. Neon reflections crawl across the ceiling in slow, distorted patterns. Arden is asleep against my chest, her breathing shallow at first, then gradually evening out. The kind of sleep that comes from exhaustion, not peace.

I don't move. I learned a long time ago that stillness keeps you sharper. It lets you notice what doesn't belong.

My phone sits face down on the coffee table. Not because it's quiet, but because every vibration feels like a fuse is being lit. The fallout is already in motion; I can feel it. You don't spend years navigating this industry without learning the rhythm of a scandal.

The first wave is chaos.

The second is control.

That's where we are now: studios are scrambling, comment sections are frozen, publicists are rewriting history in real time. Luke will be condemned loudly and cautiously, in that order. Everyone will pretend they didn't know until the moment knowing became unavoidable.

No one wants answers. They want deniability.

Arden doesn't see any of that, and I won't be the one to put it on her shoulders. She already made the hard choice. Everything after that is just the machine doing what it was built to do.

Outside, traffic hums below us, steady and indifferent. The sound of cars passing, horns honking, sirens wailing, they all blend into a sort of white noise that I've grown used to.

That's when I hear it again. The motorcycle.

That's the third time in the past hour.

The engine is a low rumble. It doesn't roar, doesn't speed past. It slows beneath the building, idles just long enough to be noticed, then moves on.

I don't get up. Don't look out the window. I already know.

Sebastian has never been subtle, but he's never been careless either. His recklessness is calculated. It's been earned through years of surviving the kinds of situations other people stumble blindly into. Parties, fights, messes he should've left alone, but didn't. That's how he learned where the edges are. How close you can get before you're in too deep.

I haven't seen him in weeks, not really. The last time we spoke face-to-face was when I caught him lurking in the stairwell like the angel of death. He hasn't tried to call or text. He's only been present when I needed him, at the hotel. Honestly, that tells me more than a conversation would.

It means something's unresolved.

Or worse, something is going on behind the scenes that he hasn't told me yet.

Arden shifts against me, exhaling softly, and I tighten my arm around her. It's almost a reflex now. Whatever Sebastian is up to can stay out there with him. Tonight, my job is here.

Minutes pass. Maybe more. Time blurs when you're the only one awake in the middle of the night. That's when I hear it. Not on the street this time; at the door.

Not a knock. Not footsteps.

Just the faintest sound of a scrape against wood. So soft it would go undetected under normal circumstances. But tonight isn't normal, and I'm on high alert.

I ease Arden gently back against the cushions, careful not to wake her, and stand. Every muscle in my body is already primed as I move toward the door. I pause, pressing my ear to the door to listen again. Nothing. I glance through the peephole. The hallway is empty and entirely too still.

I open the door anyway, stepping out into the hall. I turn to scan the hallway leading to the elevator. Then, I turn around, inspecting the stairwell longer than necessary. Still nothing.

For the first time tonight, I wonder if I should get some sleep. Hearing noises isn't exactly a good sign.

As I turn back toward the door, something catches my eye that I don't remember seeing before. A single folded piece of paper on the floor. I lean down to pick it up, and make my way back through the door, locking the deadbolt before unfolding it.

There, scrawled across the paper in red ink, are five simple words:

DO YOU MISS ME LEXI?

ACKNOWLEDGMENTS

To my husband, thank you for supporting every wild idea I bring to you, especially this one. The one that lasted far longer than a day and came with far too many sleepless nights. Thank you for always being the first to read my spicy scenes and for giving me the male perspective when I need it. I love you. In every timeline and every life.

To my children, you are the reason I wake up at the ass crack of dawn every morning, end the reason I get out of bed at all on the hardest days. You have always been worth it. If you learn anything from me, I hope it's to follow your dreams. No matter how impossible they seem

To the Core Four, you know who you are. Thank you for being chaotic, unhinged, and somehow deeply focused all at once. I would not be here without you — truly. I would have given up after the first draft. Is it strange to say I love you? Because I do. Very much.

www.ingramcontent.com/pod-product-compliance
Ingram Content Group UK Ltd.
Pitfield, Milton Keynes, MK11 3LW, UK
UKHW040238250426
12048UKWH00043B/1576